2−

Greetings!

by Tom Dudzick

A SAMUEL FRENCH ACTING EDITION

SAMUEL
FRENCH
FOUNDED 1830

NEW YORK HOLLYWOOD LONDON TORONTO

SAMUELFRENCH.COM

ISBN 978-0-573-69257-4   Printed in U.S.A.   #9704

MUSIC USE NOTE

IMPORTANT BILLING AND CREDIT REQUIREMENTS

GREETINGS! premiered at the George Street Playhouse in New Brunswick, New Jersey. The performance was directed by Gregory S. Hurst, with sets by Atkin Pace, costumes by Barbara Forbes, and lighting by Donald Holder. The Production Stage Manager was Thomas L. Clewell. The cast was as follows:

ANDY GORSKI	Mark Shannon
RANDI STEIN	Barbara Gulan
EMILY GORSKI	Beth Fowler
PHIL GORSKI	John Ramsey
MICKEY GORSKI	Patrick Kerr

GREETINGS! was subsequently produced by Arthur Cantor and Carol Ostrow at the John Houseman Theatre in New York City. The performance was directed by Dennis Začek, with costumes and sets by Bruce Goodrich, lighting by Deborah Constantine, and sound by One Dream. The Production Stage Manager was Thomas L. Clewell. The cast was as follows:

ANDY GORSKI	Gregg Edelman
RANDI STEIN	Toby Poser
EMILY GORSKI	Lenore Loveman
PHIL GORSKI	Darren McGavin
MICKEY GORSKI	Aaron Goodwin

CHARACTERS

ANDY GORSKI - 33 years old
RANDI STEIN - Andy's fiance, 29 years old
PHIL GORSKI - Andy's father, mid-60's
EMILY GORSKI - Andy's mother, mid-60's
MICKEY GORSKI - Andy's brother, 30 years old

SETTING

The play's action takes place in the Gorski household in Pittsburgh, PA.
The year is 1990.

This play may be performed with or without an intermission. If an intermission is used, it would come at the end of Scene 2, after Emily faints.

DIRECTOR'S NOTE

Playwright Steve Carter was present at the New York opening of Tom Dudzick's *Greetings!* When I chatted with him after the show about his impression of the play, he told me that it reminded him of the profile of Dizzie Gillespie's horn. I thought this a wonderful comparison, as one of the most vital aspects of *Greetings!* (like the signature of Mr. Gillespie's horn) is its ability to surprise an audience. As spectators settle in for what seems to be an amusing and perhaps comfortably familiar situation, they are lifted into another area of reflection.

In the Russian language, there are two words that resemble each other. These words are "Tsirk" and "Tserkov" which translate into English as Circus and Church, and much of Russian theater is an effective blend of these two arenas. Occasionally, an American playwright emerges who creates a work that entertains while recognizing a spirituality in the midst of chaos. Tom Dudzick has accomplished just that. He has chosen to present us with a contemporary play in which miracles occur. The time of the event is the Christmas season, which seems an appropriate choice. At a time when people spend enormous amounts of time, energy and money celebrating the season, many seem to forget or simply ignore the soul and spirituality.

Greetings! is loaded with humor and it certainly has a happy ending. Consequently, it is perceived as a comedy; however, the work offers actors the possibility of exploring the emotional as well as the comedic. Mr. Dudzick is an actor turned playwright and he has created a work in which the dialogue and behavior of the characters is rooted in humanity. Tom Dudzick's message may seem out of place to the cynical and jaded, but it is a play brimming with good nature and positive outlook.

–Dennis Začek
Artistic Director
Victory Gardens Theater
Chicago, 1994

To Holly.

Scene 1

(The Gorski household, nestled in a working class neigh-borhood of Pittsburgh, PA. A modest dwelling; no rich people here. The dining room table is covered with a Christmas tablecloth from Woolworths and a poinsettia plant from the A&P. Next to the living room window stands a partially decorated Christmas tree. Colored lights are strung around all the windows, but they're not plugged in.)

(A man sits on the floor arranging the miniature figures of a manger scene. This is **MICKEY***, thirty years old and severely retarded; his mental age being about three years old. We'll come to find that his vocabulary is composed of only a small handful of words. Most of his commu-nicating is done by cheerful grunts, noises and finger pointing. He is consistently good natured.)*

*(***EMILY GORSKI***, in her 60's, enters from the kitchen with a stack of dinner plates and goes to an open door-way which leads to the basement.)*

EMILY. *(Into the basement doorway.)* I don't think it would be very nice to be sitting down there when the kids show up. *(She goes to the dining room table.)*

MAN'S VOICE. *(From the basement.)* I'm not sitting down here.

EMILY. *(Not hearing him, she continues while setting the table.)* I'm sure *her* father wasn't drinking beer in the base-ment the first time Andy paid a call.

MAN'S VOICE. *(Still downstairs.)* I'm not drinking beer. Will you hold your horses?

EMILY. If you ask me, it doesn't make a very nice first impression.

MAN'S VOICE. I'm coming, I'm coming!

EMILY. *(To herself.)* 'Course no one ever asks me.

(EMILY goes to a small table lamp near the front door, turns it on and-WHOOPS! The whole house is plunged into darkness.) Oops.

MAN'S VOICE. Jesus H. Christ!

EMILY. Sorry.

MAN'S VOICE. What'd you do?

EMILY. What?

MAN'S VOICE. What did you do?

EMILY. I turned on a lamp.

MAN'S VOICE. Which one? Where?

EMILY. What?

MAN'S VOICE. Which one?

EMILY. The pretty one.

MAN'S VOICE. Oh, the pretty one... Alright, wait a while, willya?

(The street lamp outside throws a little bit of light into the room.)

EMILY. Mama did it again, huh Mickey?

MICKEY. *(Noncommittally.)* Nnn.

EMILY. You're doing a nice job, hon'.

MICKEY. Nnn.

(In the near darkness she continues to set the table.)

EMILY. *(Calls out to the basement.)* That turkey in the fridge is going to spoil.

MAN'S VOICE. Wait a while, willya?

(The lights come on.)

EMILY. *(Calls out.)* They're on!

MAN'S VOICE. No kidding.

EMILY. *(Carefully studies Mickey at the manger scene.)* Doing the manger, huh Mickey?

MICKEY. Nnn.

EMILY. Looks nice. *(Moves to him.)* Real pretty, honey. *(Sits on nearby footstool.)* ...Mickey?

MICKEY. Nnn.

EMILY. *(Gently.)* Mickey, look at me.

(**MICKEY** *turns to her.*)

EMILY. Greetings.

MICKEY. *(Noncommittally.)* Nnn.

EMILY. Greetings. *(She's trying to get him to say it.)* Greetings.

(**MICKEY** *stares at her. She may as well be speaking Sanskrit.*)

EMILY. Come on, you can say it. Greetings.

(**MICKEY** *giggles.*)

EMILY. Come on, hon.

PHIL. (**PHIL GORSKI** *appears in the basement doorway, carrying a shopping bag of Christmas ornaments.*) Will you knock that off?

(**PHIL** *is a big man in his 60's. Looks like he may have been an athlete at one time. Now, however, when he moves about it's with the aid of a cane, limping very noticeably.* **PHIL** *'s hobby is griping to himself*)

EMILY. You hush. Mickey... greetings.

PHIL. You sound like a draft notice, cut it out.

EMILY. He said it once, he can do it again.

PHIL. Mick, take these here, willya?

MICKEY. Oh boy! *(Jumps up and goes to* **PHIL.***)*

PHIL. The last of the ornaments, put them by the tree.

MICKEY. *(Looks in the bag.)* Wow! *(A gale of laughter as he pulls out a string of garland.)*

PHIL. Yeah, wait a while, though; put it by the tree.

MICKEY. Wow! *(Chortling gleefully.* **MICKEY** *takes the bag and sits on the floor next to the tree.*)

PHIL. I'm going to call that electrician, Christmas or not, and he's going to come over and do the job right.

EMILY. *(Going back to dinner table.)* Then call the plumber while you're at it

PHIL. No, not the toilet.

(She nods.)

PHIL. Those bums. They can all take and rub rock salt.

EMILY. I better make a "jiggle the handle" sign before the kids get here.

PHIL. How many of their brats do we have to put through college before they do something right? *(Shutting basement door.)* I should've had my head examined, buying this house. Lousy wiring. And this steep stairway. I almost broke my neck just now. The guy was drunk who designed this house.

EMILY. *(Setting table.)* Well, nobody told you to move out of the old house. The old house was well made. You're the one who wanted to move; get out of that neighborhood. And if you don't like the basement, why do you spend so much time down there?

PHIL. *(To himself.)* Three guesses. *(He limps slowly over to the front door. On the way he stops to flex his leg. grimacing with pain.)* Mmph! ...What time they getting here?

EMILY. I want to ask Andy about Mickey's behavior.

PHIL. What behavior?

EMILY. He's sharp. He may be able to shed some light on it

PHLL. What behavior? He didn't do anything.

EMILY. He's acting strange.

PHLL. He's retarded, he's supposed to act strange.

MICKEY. *(Discovering a new ornament in the bag.)* Oh boy!

PHLL.. In a minute, Mick... What time they getting here?

EMILY. I mean he's acting strangely for Mickey. And what about "greetings"?

PHLL. He never said that. You're bugs.

EMILY. Well, I don't think that's very nice.

PHLL. Mick, you're all right, aintcha?

MICKEY. Oh boy!

PHLL. I spend more time with him than you do, and he hasn't done anything strange.

EMILY. *(Exiting into kitchen.)* Fine, don't listen to me.

PHIL. *(Shouts.)* What time are Andy and what's-her-name getting here?

EMILY. *(Shouts back.)* I don't know, I don't know! I lost Andy's letter, alright?

PHLL... Lost his letter? Are you sure he's coming today? Not Arbor Day?

(She enters with more table stuff.)

PHIL. Why didn't he want me to pick him up at the airport?

EMILY. He said he wanted to take a taxi. He can afford them now.

PIIL. They'll rob him blind; they're all thieves. Probably wants to impress the girl.

EMILY. She has a name. It's Randi.

PHIL. Andy and Randi, how could I forget? Randi what?

EMILY. What?

PHIL. Randi what?

EMILY. I don't know Randi what?

PHIL. Well, did he tell you anything about her? Randi's a boy's name, are you sure he's not bringing home a boy?

EMILY. Just that he's very fond of her, that's all I know.

PHIL. Well, if two men step out of that cab I'm kicking them both down the stairs. *(Goes to front door, opens it and picks up electric cord from front step. Now he notices his street.)* This is a disgrace. Y'know that, Mick?

MICKEY. Nnn.

PHIL. It's a disgrace. Look at that. One... two... three... and ours. Only four houses with lights in the windows. Are they atheists or what? Atheists, heathens, who knows anymore? They've lost the meaning of Christmas, that's all I know.... Hey, Mick! Here, plug this in.

MICKEY. Oh boy! *(Joins **PHIL** at the door and takes cord. He plugs it in and colored bulbs light up in every window.)* Wow!

PHIL. Wow is right!

EMILY. That's so pretty.

PHIL. Yeah, but how many families do you think bothered to put up lights on this street? Four. It's a disgrace. *(Shouts to street.)* It's a disgrace!

EMILY. Please, don't start on the neighbors. If they didn't feel like it, they didn't feel like it; what can you do?

PHIL. ... It's going to kill them to spend a couple bucks? Look at the Keatings. Nothing. Steve Sendecki, Joe Guzdeck. Not one lousy bulb, and you think they don't have money? Don't let them kid you.

EMILY. Please, I don't want to hear about the neighbors, not today. *(She exits into kitchen.)*

PHIL. *(To himself.)* Sure, you don't care, what do you care? Nobody cares anymore. *(Goes to his easy chair near the tree.)* Nobody cares about Christmas, Mick.

MICKEY. Nnn.

PHIL. Nobody cares about Christmas. *(He eases himself into his chair, a painful operation.)* Mmph! Gimme gimme gimme. That's all you hear. Everybody's out for themselves.

MICKEY. *(Holds up a bulb.)* Wow!

PHIL ...Okay, Mick, dump it right here. Come on.

MICKEY. Yay! *(Joyfully dumps out the ornaments onto the rug.)*

PHIL. ... Neat though, Mick, neat. Careful now.

(**MICKEY** *is giggling gleefully.* **PHIL** *points to a bulb with his cane.)*

PHIL. Here, this one.

(**MICKEY** *picks one up.)*

PHIL. No, that's broken.

MICKEY. Ah, phooey.

PHIL. See, you broke one.

MICKEY. Ah, phooey.

PHIL. ... Ah, phooey, that's right. Here, this one.

(**MICKEY** *carefully takes it, and with the utmost care he hangs it on a vacant branch.*)

PHIL. Attaboy.

(**MICKEY** *lets out a blast of laughter.* **PHIL** *can't help but laugh along.*)

PHIL. Here, this one now.

(**MICKEY** *repeats the process.*)

PHIL. You sure get a kick out of Christmas, don'tcha Mick? God bless ya. I did, too. And we didn't have nothin'. Back then we had nothin', Mick.

MICKEY. Nnn.

PHIL. I'd be happy with a set of Lincoln Logs on Christmas. Which I never got anyway. *(Pushes an ornament to* **MICKEY** *with his cane.)* Not like these kids today. Gimme this, gimme that. Not us. The Depression, Mick.

MICKEY. Nnn.

PHIL. We used to take out the garbage, then bring it back into the house and eat it again.... Mick, "how are ya?"

MICKEY. Nnn.

PHIL. Can you say that, Mick? How are ya?

MICKEY. Hiya.

PHIL. No, Mick, how are ya?

MICKEY. Hiya.

PHIL. *(Checks over his shoulder to make sure* **EMILY***'s not around.)* Mickey ... greetings.

MICKEY. Nnn.

PHIL. Can you say that, Mick? Greetings.

MICKEY. Nnn.

PHIL. Greetings.

MICKEY. Nnn.

PHIL. She's bugs.

EMILY. *(Enters and sees the tree.)* Oh, that's real pretty, Mickey. Nice, hon. *(Sees the manger scene.)* Oh, Mickey, you've got the animals wrong. *(Gets down on her knees and fiddles* *with the animals.)* Here, Mickey, see? You've got to turn the cows this way. They were breathing on the Baby Jesus. See? They kept him warm with their breath.

PHIL. You were there?

EMILY. Yes, I was there. I saw the whole thing.

PHIL. Ever have a cow breathe on you?

EMILY. I have, as a matter of fact. And it was very warm.

PHIL. Y'got your miniature cow flops in there?

(No response from **EMILY**. *She gets up from her work.)*

PHIL. Jeez, at least laugh at my jokes.

EMILY. That wasn't funny. *(she heads for the kitchen and exits.)*

PHIL. Mick, I give up.

MICKEY. Nnn.

PHIL. She used to laugh at my jokes.

EMILY. *(***EMILY** *sticks her head back in.)* Are you going to get the electric trains? Andy likes to set them up.

PHIL. If Andy wants them he can get them. I'm tired.

*(***EMILY** *shrugs and exits.)*

PHIL. He'll have plenty of strength after that relaxing cab ride. *(A long silence. Then* **PHIL** *leans on his cane and pulls himself to his feet.)* Let's go get the trains, Mick.

MICKEY. Oh boy! *(***MICKEY** *jumps up, runs to the basement door and opens it.)*

PHIL. Whoa, whoa, whoa, hold your horses, willya?

*(***MICKEY** *laughs.)*

PHIL. Turn the light on first. Take it slow on them stairs.

*(***MICKEY** *turns on the basement light and disappears down the stairs.* **PHIL** *follows him down.)*

PHIL. Guy goes out on a five day drunk, then designs this house. Oughta have my head examined. *(And he's gone.)*

(A moment goes by, then **EMILY** *enters with some more stuff for the dinner table. She sees the open basement door and goes to it.)*

EMILY. *(Into the basement.)* You said no more beer.

PHIL'S VOICE. *(Shouts.)* I'm getting the trains!

EMILY. Oh. *(Goes to the table and busies herself.)*

> *(Now the front door is opened by* **ANDY,** *33, and* **RANDI,** *30, dressed for winter and carrying luggage. They enter quietly and set down their bags.* **ANDY** *gestures that* **RANDI** *be silent.)*

> *(With her back to them,* **EMILY** *hears nothing. They stand and watch as* **EMILY** *fusses at the table. Finally,* **EMILY** *exits into the kitchen.)*

ANDY. Mrs. Clause. Pittsburgh's answer to June Cleaver.

RANDI. She's so cute! And a little hard of hearing?

ANDY. Uh-huh. So, it's not too late, we could still turn around and go back to New York.

RANDI. Stop that.

ANDY. *(Takes a deep breath for courage.)* Okay... ready if you are. *(He opens the front door, slams it as if they've just arrived, and noisily drops his bag.)* Well, well, well!

> *(***EMILY** *comes out of the kitchen and goes to them, all smiles.)*

EMILY. Well, well, well!

ANDY. *(Arms open.)* Mama! Merry Christmas!

EMILY. *(Hugging and kissing.)* Merry Christmas!

ANDY. You look wonderful!

EMILY. Oh, sure I do!

ANDY. You do! Now, Mom... this is Randi.

RANDI. Nice to meet you, Mrs. Gorski.

ANDY. Louder.

RANDI. Nice to meet you, Mrs. Gorski.

EMILY. *(Slaps* **ANDY***'s arm.)* I heard her the first time; what'dya tell her, I was deaf?

ANDY. No, I just thought–

EMILY. You thought, you thought. Nice to meet you, too, Randi. I can hear when I pay attention; don't listen to him

RANDI. I won't.

EMILY. Take off your things, stay awhile.

(Through this next there is business of removing coats and boots and hanging them in the closet.)

ANDY. Mom, why is he- *(Checks around for PHIL.)* why is he still putting up those stupid lights?! He's gonna kill himself!

EMILY. Try and talk sense to your father.

RANDI. You have a really pretty home, Mrs. Gorski.

EMILY. What?

RANDI. *(Louder.)* You have a really pretty home.

EMILY. Oh, thank you.

RANDI. It's so nice to get out of a cramped apartment for a while.

EMILY. I'll bet.

ANDY. Where's Dad?

EMILY. In the basement.

ANDY. How is he?

EMILY. Oh, y'know. The same.

RANDI. *(Quietly.)* What does that mean, the same?

ANDY. It means Christmas is cancelled.

EMILY. Now Andy, before I can get interrupted, let me tell you about Mickey.

ANDY. What about Mickey?

EMILY. And this is a lulu.

(Now MICKEY enters from the basement with a large box of electric trains. He sees ANDY.)

MICKEY. *(Joyously.)* Oh, no!!

ANDY. Oh, yes! There's Lulu now!

MICKEY. *(Quickly sets box down on floor.)* Oh, no!

ANDY. M'main bro'!

MICKEY. Hiya! *(With a big laugh he runs to ANDY and hugs him.)*

ANDY. Hiya! How are ya, pal? *(Suddenly.)* Whoa, Jesus!

(**MICKEY** *doesn't know his own strength. He lets go.*) You're out of shape, Mick, that used to hurt.... Mickey, this is Randi.

(**MICKEY** *runs to hug her.* **ANDY** *quickly intercepts.*)

ANDY. A handshake, Mick.

(**MICKEY** *extends his hand.* **RANDI** *takes it.*)

RANDI. Hello, Mickey. Nice to meet you. Oh, I brought you something. (*Takes something from her pocket and hides it behind her back.*) I got this especially for you. Which hand?

MICKEY. Nnn.

RANDI. C'mon, which hand?

MICKEY. Nnn. ..

RANDI. (*To* **ANDY.**) Should I be doing this?

ANDY. Which hand, Mick?

MICKEY. Nnn.

ANDY. Okay, I guess he doesn't want it.

(**MICKEY** *quickly points to one of her hands.*)

ANDY. A-ha!

(**RANDI** *gives* **MICKEY** *a small bag of peanuts.*)

MICKEY. Oh boy!

EMILY. Oh boy!

ANDY. Airline peanuts, Mick!

EMILY. From an airplane, Mickey.

MICKEY. (*Examines it closely.*) He-e-ey!

EMILY. Not before dinner, honey. Thank you, Randi.

RANDI. (*Dismisses it*) Oh...

MICKEY. (*Suddenly remembers something.*) Oh-ohoh-oh...! (*Pulls a folded piece of newspaper out of his shirt pocket and gives it to* **RANDI.**)

RANDI. (*Looks at it.*) Um... wrestling matches?

MICKEY. (*Shouts, startling* **RANDI.**) Oh boy!

ANDY. Dad's taking you to the wrestling matches?

MICKEY. Oh boy!

ANDY. Or are you *in* the wrestling matches?

MICKEY. Oh boy!

ANDY. That's what I thought. *(With an evil gleam in his eye, he begins to stalk* **MICKEY.***)* Yes, ladies and gentlemen, tonight it's a tag team match between Fritz Von Erik, Haystack Calhoun, the Gallagher Brothers and a couple of midgets thrown in for laughs...

*(***MICKEY** *runs around the room, hardly able to contain his glee. He knows what's coming.* **ANDY** *approaches stealthily. }*

ANDY. The mighty Fritz Von Erik approaches his opponent with a lust for blood in his eye. He's sizing him up now. The crowd is tense... Haystack, your shoe's untied!

*(***MICKEY** *looks at his shoe and* **ANDY** *rushes him. Through this next he wrestles* **MICKEY** *to the ground;* **MICKEY** *shrieking with laughter.)*

ANDY. And Von Erik's got him in a half Nelson and an Ozzie Nelson, and a Ricky and a David! And now, can it be? Has he no mercy? Yes, folks,there it is-the paralyzer *claw!*

*(***MICKEY** *goes wild as* **ANDY** *triumphantly raises a gnarly claw for all the arena to see.)*

ANDY. The crowd goes wild! Will he? Will he? *Yeees!!*

(And finally, **ANDY** *plunges the horrible claw into* **MICKEY***'s stomach. tickling him unmercifully.)*

(Now **PHIL** *makes his appearance in the basement doorway, carrying a box of train equipment.)*

PHIL. The winner and still champeen!

ANDY. *(Gets up.)* Hey, there he is. How are you, Dad? *(Goes to* **PHIL.** *puts out his hand.)* Good to see you.

PHIL. *(Shakes his hand.)* Right-o. How are ya, good to see ya.

(A slightly uncomfortable pause.)

ANDY. I see you got out your ladder again. The lights look great.

PHIL. Yeah. But how many families do you think even bothered to put up lights? Guess.

EMILY. Phil.

PHIL. What!

ANDY. That ladder is in good shape, isn't it, Dad?

PHIL. Yeah, yeah, yeah, you sound like your mother. Here. *(Hands him the box.)* Ghosts of Christmas past.

ANDY. Hey, the good old Lionel, Mick!

MICKEY. Oh boy!

(**ANDY** *joins* **MICKEY** *on the floor and* **THEY** *examine the box's contents.*)

PHIL. What did you pay for that cab?

ANDY. What? Oh,l don't know.

PHIL. What do you mean, you don't know? It wasn't free, was it?

ANDY. Well, I don't know ... twenty, twenty-two, something like that So, how are you doing?

PHIL. Jesus Christ! I coulda picked you up for nothing. What're you, goofy?

ANDY. No, it's no problem. I'm used to taking cabs, that's all. New Yorkers live in them.

PHIL. *(Reaches for wallet.)* Here, take twenty.

ANDY. No, don't be silly, it's fine.

PHIL. Take it and shut up, willya?

ANDY. No, Dad, come on. I take cabs all the time.

EMILY. Phil.

PHIL. What! You want people to think I'm a bum?

EMILY. I won't tell a soul.

ANDY. *(Rises and heads for* **RANDI.**) We'll discuss the twenty after dinner, I promise, okay? Right now I'd like to introduce you to a friend of mine.

(**RANDI** *reacts to "friend."*)

ANDY. Dad, this is Randi.

PHIL. Hi, how are ya? I just don't want you to think I'm a bum, that's all.

RANDI. I'd never think such a thing. *(With a look to* **ANDY.***)* What kind of "friend" would I be?

ANDY. Well no, I meant... y'know...

RANDI. It's nice to finally meet you, Mr. Gorski. I've heard so much about you.

PHIL. *(A look to* **ANDY.***)* Oh?

EMILY. Come on, folks, sit, sit.

> *(***PHIL** *sits in his easy chair. On her way to sofa* **RANDI** *gives* **MICKEY** *his wrestling ad.)*

MICKEY. Oh boy! *(Puts it back in his pocket.)*

ANDY. *(Moving to couch, picks up shopping bag.)* Christmas presents, Mick.

MICKEY. Oh no! *(Runs to* **ANDY.***)*

ANDY. Oh yes!

> *(***MICKEY** *takes presents to the tree and through this next quietly arranges them.)*

EMILY. *(Sitting.)* I hope you like meat loaf, Randi.

RANDI. Love it.

EMILY. And baked apples for dessert.

RANDI. Mmm!

EMILY. Then on Christmas we're having the Christmas turkey.

ANDY. Good planning.

EMILY. Can I get you anything right now? A drink?

RANDI. No, thank you. I had a drink on the plane.

PHIL. How much did they charge you?

RANDI. Nothing. It was complimentary.

EMILY. Andy, a drink?

ANDY. No thanks, Mom.

PHIL. Andy, y'might as well plug in the tree, we've been saving that for you.

ANDY. I'd be honored.

PHIL. Mickey's been working on it all day.

ANDY. You decorate a mean tree, Fritz.

(MICKEY laughs. ANDY plugs in the tree. The lights flash on for a split second, sparks fly out of the wall socket, ANDY yelps, and the tree goes DARK.)

PHIL. Jesus H. Christ! ...Unplug it, unplug it.

EMILY. Careful, Andy!

ANDY. I know, I know. *(He carefully unplugs the tree. To RANDI.)* At midnight we blow up the train. *(He heads back to the couch.)*

EMILY. When are you going to try a different electrician?

PHIL. He is going to do the job right! Now let's drop it.

EMILY. Fine.

ANDY. ...Merry Christmas. *(Sits.)*

PHIL. Randi.

RANDI. Yes.

PHIL. How'd you end up with a boy's name?

RANDI. It's a girl's name, too. Randi with an i.

PHIL. I never heard it.

EMILY. I like it. *(Sing-song.)* Andy and Randi, Andy and Randi.

ANDY. *(Nicely.)* Don't do that.

PHIL. What's your last name?

ANDY. Gorski.

PHIL. Not yours. I know yours.

RANDI. Stein.

PHIL. Huh?

RANDI. Stein.

EMILY. How was your flight?

ANDY. *(Grateful for the change of subject.)* Fine. Real good. No delays. Just fine. Good peanuts... Honey roasted.

RANDI. *(To PHIL.)* I'm Jewish.

PHIL. Huh? Yeah, well I figured. Stein, that's a Jewish name.

EMILY. You're sure I can't get you a drink?

RANDI. No, I'm fine.

ANDY. We're fine, Mom.

PHIL. You don't have Christmas, huh?

RANDI. Nope.

ANDY. She has New Year's.

PHIL. No kidding.... You have Chanukah, right?

RANDI. No, actually I don't have much of anything, holiday-wise.

PHIL. No holidays? Come on, you're loaded with holidays. Even I know that. Bernie Fine, remember Bernie Fine, Emily?

EMILY. Sure.

PHIL. Used to come into the store, always celebrating something or other. Young Kipper, y'got that, dont'cha?

RANDI. I don't celebrate it.

ANDY. It's "Yom Kippur."

PHIL. Gee, excuse me.... You don't celebrate that?

RANDI. No.

PHIL. Mm-hmm. *(To* **EMILY.***)* What else did Bernie used to celebrate? I forget.

EMILY. I don't know, but whenever anyone in his family died he used to sit and shiver and I never knew why.

ANDY. *(More to himself.)* ...Yep ...Honey roasted

PHIL. *(To* **RANDI.***)* So, no kiddin', Chanukah's out?

RANDI. Chanukah's out.

PHIL. I don't get it; how come? That's twelve presents, right? They got it from the twelve days of Christmas.

ANDY. It's eight presents.

RANDI. Mr. Gorski, to me Chanukah is eight days like any other.

EMILY. *(The light begins to dawn.)* We have white wine, red wine, beer, Dr. Pepper ...

(**ANDY** *gestures "no thanks."*)

(*A pause.*)

PHIL. Rosha somethin' ... Shogun.

(**RANDI** *gestures no.*)

ANDY. Dad, Randi's an atheist.

PHIL. Oh, oh! ...Oh. *(That last "oh" speaks volumes.)*

(There is a lo-o-ng silence.)

EMILY. *(Finally.)* Andy, how's the job?

ANDY. Oh... same... How's housework?

EMILY. Oh, 'bout the same.

ANDY. Dad, how's retirement?

PHIL. Stinko.

EMILY. *(Suddenly.)* Oh, Andy, I almost called you on the phone, I was so excited! Your new commercial!

ANDY. New commercial?

EMILY. I never saw anything like it! That sunset and those running horses on the beach, and the orchestra playing. It was... inspirational!

ANDY. For the laxative.

EMILY. For the laxative.

ANDY. *(Ahem.)* No, Steve Smith did that.

EMILY. Oh.

ANDY. I didn't get that.

EMILY. Oh.

PHIL. What do you do for a living?

ANDY. *(Jovially; anything to stall.)* I write ad copy.

PHIL. *Not you!* ...Jesus, how many complimentary drinks did you have on that plane?

ANDY. Sorry.

RANDI. I'm an actress.

(This hangs in the air for a while.)

EMILY. *(Finally.)* Interesting!

RANDI. *(A little doubtful.)* I thought so.

ANDY. She's a wonderful actress.

EMILY. I'm sure she is! An actress, Phil, you hear that?

PHIL. Am I sitting here? *(To RANDI.)* Makin' any dough?

EMILY. Phil!

PHIL. What?

EMILY. Honestly!

ANDY. Well, it's a tough field.

EMILY. Of course it is.

RANDI. I did a commercial.

EMILY. TV?

RANDI. Just extra work.

ANDY. But a big client. Milk of Magnesia.

EMILY. Well, okay, that's right up our alley!

PHIL. Emily!

RANDI. But I'm afraid I didn't really answer your question. For an actual living... I waitress.

EMILY. ....Oh.

PHIL. *(Throwing in the towel.)* See if the paper's here, Mick.

> **(MICKEY** *gets up and goes to the front door. Through this next he will get the newspaper from the porch, then quietly sit on the staircase and leaf through it. looking at the pictures.)*

EMILY. Where are you from, Randi?

RANDI. You mean what planet?

EMILY. *(Confused.)* What?

RANDI. I'm from Rome.

PHIL & EMILY. Rome?

ANDY. Rome, New York.

PHIL & EMIL Y. Oh.

EMILY. And what do your folks do?

RANDI. *(Hesitantly.)* I don't know.

PHIL. You don't know?

RANDI. I mean I'm not sure what they do now. My father's retired, so I guess he putters. And my mother... well, she used to like to join clubs, so... I guess she's still joining.

PHIL. You guess?

RANDI. I don't get home much.

(Another awkward pause.)

ANDY. *(To the rescue.)* Dad! Randi's father used to watch you play ball!

PHIL. You're kiddin'.

RANDI. No! He spent one summer in Pittsburgh before he married my mom, and he used to go to the ball games. Especially the minors, 'cause he loved to watch Georgie Thurman.

PHIL. Ho! Who didn't?

RANDI. But that's where he saw you pitch.

PHIL. *(To EMILY.)* Boy, Georgie Thurman. Great catcher! There's a guy who took off.... So, you're old man was a fan, huh?

RANDI. A fanatic. Thurman, Gonzales and Gorski—he never stopped talking about that minor league team. He said you were great

PHIL. ....Yeah. 'Course we were all just a bunch of bums in those days. Not like today with your superstars and your billion dollar contracts and your cocaine addicts. No, we only had one addiction back then. Baseball. *(Calls out.)* Mick, the paper!

   (MICKEY gets up.)

RANDI. How long did you play ball?

PHIL. Oh, gee, I dunno...

ANDY. Dad had to stop when he broke his hip.

PHIL. Yeah, I broke my hip.

RANDI. Oh, that's too bad. How did that happen?

PHIL. Got hit by a car.

EMILY. Hit by a car.

ANDY. Hit by a car.

RANDI. Oh...

   (MICKEY comes in and hands paper to PHIL. He sits on floor.)

EMILY. Oh! Now let me tell you! *(To* **PHIL.***)* And you hush up. This is my story. *(To* **ANDY.***)* Guess who looked me straight in the eye and said the word "greetings."

PHIL. He did not.

EMILY. Now shut up! I'm telling this. *(To* **ANDY.***)* Take a guess.

ANDY. *(A long blank look.)* The mailman.

EMILY. Oh, Andy, come on.

ANDY. Well, he's so morose.

RANDI. *(Taking a guess.)* Mickey.

ANDY. No, not Mickey.

EMILY. Yes!

ANDY. What?!

(**PHIL** *gets up with a disapproving grunt.*)

EMILY. *(A warning to* **PHIL.***)* Hey...!

(**PHIL** *continues to sideboard and makes himself a drink.*)

ANDY. Mickey said "greetings"?

EMILY. As clear as a bell.

(**ANDY** *looks at* **MICKEY** *in wonder.*)

ANDY. *(To* **EMILY.***)* Greetings?

EMILY. Greetings.

ANDY. *(At a loss. He turns to* **RANDI.***)* Greetings.

RANDI. I take it this is unusual.

ANDY. "Oh boy" and "wow." That has been it.

EMILY. *(A look to* **PHIL.***)* Now, if I can tell this without interruption… Your brother's been acting strange these last couple weeks. He sits and stares into space for ten, fifteen minutes at a time. No rocking, just sitting perfectly still.

(**ANDY** *watches as* **MICKEY** *gently rocks back and forth; something he does while sitting quietly.*)

EMILY. Then I'd call him or touch him, and he'd snap right out of it. So I didn't worry about it. Daydreaming, I figured. Well, then, the day before yesterday I was out there cleaning the oven, and Mickey's sitting at the kitchen table watching me. I wasn't paying any attention to him, I had my head in the oven. Well, finally I pulled my head out and I said, "Help me up, Mickey." And I'll be damned if he isn't there in that trance again. So I said, "Hey, buster." And suddenly, I think I'm seeing things; his face becomes real... *(Searches for word.)* ...intelligent And that's when he comes out with it. "Greetings!" Well, boom, down I went on my fanny. Now that was two days ago and nothing's happened since.... So, what do you think?

(ANDY is dumbfounded by the story. He gets up and playfully looks MICKEY in the eye.)

MICKEY. *(With the claw.)* Rrr!

ANDY. *(Finally.)* I don't know what to think!

EMILY. *(Gestures to PHIL.)* And this one won't believe me. Thinks I'm bugs.

ANDY. Why don't you believe her, Dad?

PHIL. She had her head in the oven; she was goofy from the fumes.

EMILY. It's an electric oven.

PHIL. The cleaning fumes! Don't you think I know it's an electric oven? The cleaning fluid fumes. Breathe enough of those and you'll be having conversations with the garbage disposal, if it was working.

ANDY. Mom—

EMILY. *(To PHIL.)* I know when I'm hearing right and I was hearing right.

ANDY. Mom, I don't know. I wouldn't make too much of it.

EMILY. Why not?

ANDY. I think he just got lucky.

EMILY. Lucky?

ANDY. That's the only thing that makes sense. He hears the word on TV or someplace and then, boomph, out it comes.

EMILY. *(Shaking her head.)* Andy, you had to see his face. He was another person.

PHIL. *(Moves to cellar door.)* Mick, watch out they don't start sticking pins in you.

EMILY. Where are you going?

PHIL. What do you mean, where am I going?

EMILY. Where are you going?

PHIL. I'll tell you when I get there.

EMILY. Phil, don't.

PHIL. What!

EMILY. Just don't. All right? Don't. Dinner's going to be ready soon.

PHIL. So call me, I'll come up.

EMILY. Sure, you'll come up, all right.

PHIL. What's that mean?

EMILY. For God's sake, Phil, it's Christmas.

PHIL. Oh, that's right, it's Christmas. Do you know where I can get some cows to breathe on me? It gets cold down there. Your mother was there, you know, at the first Noel. She knows the Blessed Mother personally. That's how she got to be so perfect; she took lessons from Mary. Ask her about it.

EMILY. Phil...

PHIL. Saint Emily. They canonized her; we had a party out in the garage.

EMILY. You should hear yourself. You're ridiculous.

PHIL. I'm ridiculous?

ANDY. *(Getting to his feet.)* Um... folks, could we not do this? I know, I know, I usually don't interfere in these little sessions. But, well, it's Christmas, and... And, um... And...

PHIL. And what?

ANDY. And I asked Randi to marry me!

EMILY. What?!

PHIL. Huh?!

ANDY. I asked Randi to marry me. And not just because our names rhyme. So, uh... surprise. Heh, I realize you don't know her very well. Or at all. But, well... I love her. Not because she's beautiful, which she is. Or because she makes me laugh. Or because she makes me feel like I actually have a shot at happiness. I don't love Randi because anything. I just love her.... And I worry that if she gets the idea that we're not exactly a loving and tender and perfect family, she might change her mind about accepting my hand.

RANDI. *(Takes his hand.)* Not a chance.

(A long moment.)

PHIL. Married. Well... good luck. *(And he disappears into the basement.)*

EMILY. Well... isn't this exciting! I guess we'll have lots to talk about... Oh, my meat loaf! *(She quickly exits into the kitchen.)*

*(**ANDY** and **RANDI** are left looking at each other. They kiss.)*

MICKEY. Wow... !

(The lights fade to black.)

Scene 2

(It's an hour later. The luggage is out of sight and Everyone is seated at the dinner table. **PHIL** *and* **EMILY** *eat mechanically, deep into their own thoughts.)*

ANDY. *(Between bites.)* We actually know someone who got married underwater.

RANDI. In scuba gear.

ANDY. Seriously. I guess they had sponge cake.

RANDI. And the sky divers...

ANDY. The sky divers, right, got married in mid-air. We know a lot of weird people. But my favorite—I read about this—one couple got married while bungee-jumping. I think one of their wedding gifts was flubber... Luckily, Randi and I are a little more traditional.

RANDI. A lot more traditional.

ANDY. Yeah. We've decided to have the ceremony performed by a justice of the peace. We'd like to have you all come up for it. Y'know, meet Randi's parents. And we'll all go out to dinner afterwards. At the Plaza or someplace. You can stay over, and the next night we'll catch a Broadway show. Make a whole weekend out of it. *(Waits for a response; gets none.)* Huh, Mick?

MICKEY. Oh boy!

PHIL. Sounds expensive.

ANDY. Well, we could discuss a loan. *(The humor is lost on* **PHIL.** *Now, after an uncomfortable pause.)* Randi... tell them about your Christmas records.

RANDI. Oh, Andy, come on.

ANDY. Please?

RANDI. Andy...

ANDY. See, on the plane I was telling Randi that what I missed the most about Christmas was that delicious sense of mystery there was about the whole thing. Like, where did the presents really come from? And if Santa has elves, why does it say "Mattel"? And then Randi told me about her Christmas Albums.

RANDI. Well, I was just saying that I had these Christmas albums when I was little. Jewish or not, I loved my Christmas albums. Nat King Cole was my favorite. But for years I thought Santa Claus was an alcoholic, on account of my Nat King Cole record. See, it had a skip in it. It would go-*(Sings.)* "They know that Santa's on his way. He's loaded (click)-He's loaded (click)-He's loaded (click)—"

(**ANDY** *grins, waiting for his folks' reaction.*)

EMILY. *(Finally.)* The thing about atheists... it's always puzzled me, how you could believe that all the beauty in this world could have just happened by accident.

PHIL. Yeah, who do you think created all the beauty in the world?

(*Needless to say, it's an awkward moment.*)

ANDY. Did we just enter a time warp?

PHIL. What's the matter, I can't ask a question?

ANDY. No, hey, ask away.

EMILY. Andy...

ANDY. Yes?

EMILY. Will you consider yourself married in the eyes of God?

ANDY. Um... well... sure. I think God will be there in the judge's chambers.

EMILY. You do.

ANDY. Yeah. I don't think God cares whether we're in a church or in a judge's office or in a Dairy Queen, as long as we're sincere about what we're doing.

EMILY. Mmm... Randi, what do you think?

RANDI. I think Andy's entitled to his own beliefs.

EMILY. But you, personally. don't believe God will be there in the judge's chambers.

ANDY. Mom...

EMILY. I'm asking a question.

ANDY. Couldn't we discuss politics?

RANDI. Mrs. Gorski, I know this is unsettling for you. Are you sure you want to pursue it?

EMILY. I want to understand.

RANDI. *(A pause.)* No, I don't believe a God will be at our marriage ceremony.

PHIL. *(Rises.)* That's all. I've lost my appetite.

ANDY. Dad, come on.

PHIL. Come on what? This is blasphemous.

ANDY. It's no such thing. She has a belief and she's entitled to it.

PHIL. You go along with this?

ANDY. What do you mean, go along with this? What does that mean?

PHIL. It's not the way you were raised.

ANDY. All right, but I got over it.

PHIL. Now what does that mean?

EMILY. All right, enough you two.

PHIL. You were raised to believe in the Commandments. What's happened to that?

EMILY. Enough.

PHIL. When was the last time you took Holy Communion, tell me that.

ANDY. What does that have to do with anything?

PHIL. Are you an atheist, too, now?

ANDY. Didn't I just say I wasn't?

EMILY. Will you both cut it out? Andy's right, we're not exactly being fair to Randi.

PHIL. Oh, God forbid!—you'll pardon the expression... *(Sits.)* All right, you want me to be fair? Fine, I'll be fair. Go ahead, miss, you have the floor. Is there a God or isn't there?

RANDI. *(Calmly.)* Mr. Gorski, my beliefs aren't the issue here.

PHIL. Oh, they're not? And how's that?

RANDI. Because I don't have a problem with my beliefs. And Andy doesn't have a problem with my beliefs.

PHIL. Yes, but I do.

RANDI. That's the issue.

PHIL. What do you suggest I do about it?

ANDY. *(Amiably.)* Find a way to deal with it?

(A tense moment.)

EMILY. "White Christmas" is on tonight. Remember, Andy? *(To* **RANDI**.*)* I'd be Vera Ellen and he'd be Rosemary Clooney, and we'd sing, "Sisters... sisters..."

PHIL. Well, y'know... I feel sorry for you, miss.

ANDY. Dad.

PHIL. Because the day you die you're going to get the surprise of your life.

ANDY. Dad, come on.

RANDI. Mr. and Mrs. Gorski, if it'll help you to understand... *(A sympathetic look to* **ANDY**.*)* I'm sorry, I promised I wasn't going to start this...

PHIL. Well, we're really not that interested.

EMILY. *(Snaps.)* Can you stop for five seconds?!

RANDI. *(To* **EMILY**, *almost tenderly.)* This wasn't just a whim, my "non-belief." I didn't choose it last Spring to be fashionable. It began long ago. On my eleventh birthday. We were having a party outdoors and I watched a car jump a curb in front of my house and kill my baby sister. In my heart I couldn't justify how a God who created everything and watches over everything could permit this to happen. *(Gently to* **PHIL**.*)* You asked me who I think created all the beauty in this world. I haven't the faintest idea. But it is an odd question. Because I don't think you find the world very beautiful. I think you find it pretty stinko. Am I right?

PHIL. That's as good a word as any.

RANDI. Well, so do I sometimes. My escape is laughter. Maybe yours is God, and I think that's fine. But I have to ask–what has all this got to do with me marrying your son?

EMILY. Randi, it's just that we feel—

PHIL. No, I have to ask how you'd feel if everything you've ever believed in was suddenly tossed out with the Christmas left-overs.

ANDY. When did that happen? Nobody ever said there was anything wrong with your beliefs, or that you should stop believing what you do. I've altered my beliefs, that's all.

PHIL. So what does that say about mine?

ANDY. What? It says nothing.

PHIL. Nothing? Only that my beliefs are wrong.

ANDY. No way.

PHIL. No way? I believe one thing, you believe another. We can't both be right.

ANDY. Yes we can.

PHIL. We can? What planet have you been living on?

ANDY. It has nothing to do with right or wrong.

PHIL. I'll ask again, on what planet? You believe there's a God. She believes there is no God. Who's right?

(ANDY *doesn't answer.*)

There either is a God or there isn't. It can't be both ways. Who's right?

RANDI. (*Anything for peace, She raises her hand.*) How many hang out their flag on holidays?

(EMILY *rises and goes to sideboard for the bowl of baked apples.*)

PHIL. (*Continues to* ANDY.) You got an answer? Whose beliefs are right and whose are wrong?

ANDY. Randi's beliefs are right because they're right for her. Mine are right because they're right for me. Yours are right because—

PHIL. Bullshit! Look. See this? (*Reaches into the bowl that* EMILY *has just set down, and pulls out an apple.*) A delicious baked apple, created with a mother's tender loving care. See it? (*Keeping his eye on* ANDY *he tosses the apple over his shoulder. It hits the floor with a splat.*)

EMILY. Phil!

PHIL. I say it's in my hand. You say it's on the floor.

EMILY. I say you get a kick right in the ass! *(Through this next,* **EMILY** *goes about cleaning it up.)*

PHIL. *(Still to* **ANDY.***)* Who's right? Huh? I say it's in my hand. Am I right? Your girl friend says it's on the floor. Is she right?

ANDY. *(Getting to his feet.)* I know one thing. I was right when I said this was the wrong house to visit on Christmas.

PHIL. *(With a hurried effort he gets to his feet as well.)* You got an answer?

ANDY. Randi, I'm going to phone for a cab.

EMILY. Andy!

PHIL. Who's right, Andy?

EMILY. Phil, stop it!

PHIL. If she's right then I've been talking out of my ass for sixty-five years.

ANDY. *(To* **RANDI.***)* The bags are on the upstairs landing. Could you get them, please? *(He goes for the phone.)*

EMILY. Andy, please, sit down. Phil, you shut up.

PHIL. *(Relentless.)* If she's right then I might as well slit my throat right now. I mean, if there's no God, what's the point of going on, right Andy? Who's right, Andy?

RANDI. *(Getting up.)* Look everyone, I'm really sorry about this. Can't we just—

ANDY. You have nothing to be sorry for. Just get the bags, please.

PHIL. Oh, I see, everybody's right. The apple's on the floor, and it's in my hand. There is no God and there is a God. It has nothing to do with right and wrong.

ANDY. *(Furiously flipping through the phone book.)* I can't talk to you. Everything has to be your way or nothing.

EMILY. *(To* **PHIL.***)* Are you happy now, you big bully?

PHIL. I think he'd stick around if he had an answer for me.

ANDY. I could explain for a thousand years; you'd never understand.

PHIL. Oh, there it is. I'm stupid. I'm a stupid ballplayer. I don't live in New York and ride around in taxi cabs, so I wouldn't understand. Is that it, Andy? Is that it? Do you think I'm stupid, Andy?

(With frustration and rage, ANDY flings the phone book to the floor with an explosive "whump!")

PHIL. That doesn't answer my question, Andy.

ANDY. You want an answer?!

PHIL. I'd love one.

ANDY. You want an answer?!

PHIL. Let's hear it!

MICKEY. Greetings!

(Everyone freezes in astonished silence. For a moment the very air seems to be holding its breath. Now they slowly turn to find MICKEY, still at the dinner table, nonchalantly leaning on one elbow, and watching them all with a genial smile. Though in repose, there is an intelligence and alertness about him that we've never seen before.)

EMILY. M-Mickey?

MICKEY. Andrew, if you and your charming friend could see your way to staying, I may be able to shed some light on this right-or-wrong, God-or-no-God business. But first... a most magnificent aroma comes from yonder kitchen. Kind lady, may I trouble you for a cup of your coffee?

(Another frozen moment, then EMILY sinks to the floor in a dead faint.)

(Hardly able to take his eyes from MICKEY, ANDY goes to EMILY's aid as the lights fade to black.)

Scene 3

(A couple minutes later. **EMILY** *is seated in Phil's easy chair, just starting to regain consciousness.* **ANDY** *kneels next to her with a glass of water, rubbing her hand. While administering to his mother, however, he can't take his eyes off* **MICKEY**.*)*

(Nor can anyone else. **PHIL** *and* **RANDI** *are rooted to the spot where we saw them last; blank. utterly astonished and very shaken.)*

*(***MICKEY**, *the man of the moment, is still at the table. but seemingly back to his old self. He is complacently eating his meatloaf)*

ANDY. Mom, are you all right? Here. *(Gives her a sip of water.)*

EMILY. Thank you... I haven't done that since I was a little girl. Picking string beans in the hot sun. *(She comes fully awake and looks around. She sees* **MICKEY** *and remembers. Gasp!)* Did it really happen?

ANDY. The jury's still out

(Now **MICKEY** *puts his fork and knife neatly on his plate. He gets up and carries the plate carefully toward the kitchen. Before reaching the door he notices everyone on the other side of the room, watching his every move. He stops and looks back at them.)*

MICKEY. *(A big smile.)* Hiya! *(And he exits into the kitchen.)*

(Another moment. and everyone starts to breathe again. **PHIL** *slowly gets down on one knee, makes the sign of the cross and bows his head in silent and intense prayer.)*

RANDI. *(With a sudden laugh.)* This is an elaborate practical joke on me, right? He's been talking all his life.

*(***ANDY** *and* **EMILY** *turn and stare blankly at* **RANDI** *as her smile slowly fades.)*

ANDY. *(Valiantly fighting off panic.)* I think the best thing that we can all do right now is admit that it happened. If we—

(**MICKEY** *comes out of the kitchen. Everyone snaps to attention and watches as he casually enters the room, wiping his hands on a dish towel. On his way he passes close to* **ANDY**.)

MICKEY. *(Suddenly gives* **ANDY** *the claw.)* Rrr!

(**ANDY** *almost jumps out of his skin. Now* **MICKEY** *remembers something.*)

MICKEY. Oh-oh-oh-! *(He pulls that news ad out of his shirt pocket and shows it to* **ANDY**.)

ANDY. Wr–wrestling, Mick.

MICKEY. Oh boy!

ANDY. Next week, Mick.

MICKEY. Oh boy! *(Moves to tree.)*

ANDY. *(Gingerly approaches* **MICKEY**.) How ya doing, Mick?

MICKEY. Nnn.

ANDY. Feel all right?

MICKEY. Nnn.

ANDY. You want regular or decaf?

RANDI. Andy, don't joke.

(**ANDY** *gets up and slowly backs away from* **MICKEY**, *keeping his eye on him. Soon he starts to laugh and cry at the same time. On seeing this,* **EMILY** *starts to blubber as well. Now* **PHIL** *pulls out a hankie and starts dabbing his eyes and blowing his nose.*)

ANDY. I'm scared but I'm so excited!

PHIL. *(Through his tears.)* He talked!

EMILY. Mickey talked!

PHIL. A miracle.

EMILY. That's what it is.

PHIL. A miracle. Thank you, God.

EMILY. Thank you, God.

PHIL. Mickey, come here.

MICKEY. Nnn. *(Goes to* **PHIL**.)

PHIL. Come here, son. (*He embraces* **MICKEY**, *almost violently.*) My boy. Oh, my boy.

(**MICKEY** *just giggles.* **EMILY** *gets up and joins them in a three-way embrace.*)

EMILY. Mickey...! Here, let me look at you.

(*Sets* **MICKEY** *at arm's length and gazes at him in wonder.* **PHIL** *squeezes* **EMILY**'s *shoulder. She puts her arm around his waist and squeezes back.*)

EMILY. I gave up praying twenty-five years ago. Told myself he's never going to talk. Face facts, Emily, he's never going to be a normal boy.

PHIL. Just goes to show you.

EMILY. You must never lose faith.

PHIL. (*An arm around* **EMILY**.) Never. God has a plan.

EMILY. That's the truth.

PHIL. It may not be what we'd plan.

EMILY. But what do we know about... things?

PHIL. That's right.

(*They gaze at their son for another moment.*)

MICKEY (*Bored.*) Ah, phooey. (*He goes back to the tree and sits, playing with the trains.*)

PHIL. God is good... God is good!

(**EMILY** *sits;* **PHIL** *sits in his easy chair.*)

RANDI. (*After a respectful moment.*) Any thoughts on why God would give him an accent?

PHIL. What?

RANDI. It just seems that this could stand some examination. I mean, who am I, but...

PHIL. Examination?! Examine what?

RANDI. Well, his–his voice, his choice of words, his—

ANDY. Yeah, those words, why those words?

PHIL. Why not?

ANDY. Well, after thirty years of silence I think I would've said, "Listen, everybody, I can talk", or "Halleluliah", or... anything but that.

PHIL. You two just don't get it, do you? We are dealing here with a miracle.

ANDY. But even if it was a miracle there should be a certain logic to it. Huh? Where is the logic here? I don't see it.

PHIL. There are some things we weren't meant to understand.

ANDY. Come on Dad, you don't believe that. If that were true we wouldn't have medicine and psychiatry and airplanes. All we're asking is that this be examined a little. We owe that to Mickey, anyway. *(Sits on couch,* **RANDI** *sits with him.)* Something might be wrong with him.

(Oblivious to all this, **MICKEY** *disappears behind couch, rolling a caboose on the floor.)*

PHIL. Wrong with him? Wrong with him? *(To* **EMILY***.)* What does it take for this guy?

ANDY. There could be a psychological disorder here. Multiple personality, schizophrenia, stuff we can't even spell, I don't know, but we've got to look into it.

EMILY. *(Heads for bookshelf.)* Would "multiple personalities" be in the encyclopedia?

PHIL. What, are you listening to them, now? You people are so off base it's hilarious. *(Snaps at* **EMILY***.)* Get away from those books!

EMILY. *(Snaps back.)* What if they're right?

PHIL. Listen to me. God, in his infinite love, has smiled on this family and given us a gift. Simple. Logical. But you want to pick it apart and poke it and label it, and as sure as shooting, God is going to see that as ingratitude and he's going to take it back. I would.

ANDY. Dad, for Mickey's sake, we can't rule out the possibility of a mental disorder.

PHIL. It's not mental, it's a miracle!

MICKEY. *(Standing up from behind the sofa.)* It is a little bit of both.

(Here we go again! **RANDI** *and* **ANDY** *leap off the couch. Everyone freezes as a chill runs up and down their collective spines.)*

MICKEY. *(He proceeds with great natural charm and a certain old world formality. He does indeed have an accent, but of indeterminate origin.)* Mental in the sense that there are complex psychological maneuvers taking place at this time and miraculous in the sense that... Well, that is in the eye of the beholder, is it not? From my point of view, all of life is a miracle. Now, before we see any more fainting spells, could we be seated? *(No one moves. He gestures for everyone to take a seat.)* Dear Emily. Philip. Andrew. Chavaleh.

(Stiffly, awkwardly, everyone seats themselves.)

EMILY. *(To* **RANDI**.*)* Chavaleh?

RANDI. *(Dazed.)* My Hebrew name.

MICKEY. A little better. Now, my time with you is short. The host, though an excellent one, does have limitations in terms of duration. But in every other respect the interchange is successful, so we will be happy with that. Now—

ANDY. W–wait, wait, wait... The host?

MICKEY. Michael, your brother, who, I assure you, is resting safe and sound in a pleasant, dissociated state.

PHIL. *(Shaken.)* Mickey, please... this–this is very scary for an old man.

MICKEY. It needn't be. There is no danger as to Michael's mental or emotional stability. Nor to yours, if you would but relax.

ANDY. Wait, now... if Mickey isn't here... who are you?

MICKEY. If a name is necessary, you may call me Lucius.

PHIL. Lucius?!

ANDY. Why are you here?

LUCIUS. To settle a debt.

ANDY. To settle a debt?

LUCIUS. Be it known, it was my intention to make my magnificent appearance at that magical hour of midnight. But you rushed me, eh? Still, I hope I have brought back some of that–what did you say–that "delicious sense of mystery" that your Christmases have been lacking.

ANDY. Well, frankly... Lucius...

PHIL. His name is not Lucius. That is your brother, Mickey.

LUCIUS. I did not say it was my name. A name is not necessary to my state of being at this point. If you need a name, Lucius is suitable. It belonged to me once. She gave it to me. *(Gesturing to* **RANDI.***)*

RANDI. I-I beg your pardon?

LUCIUS. On the Isle of Crete, many, many lifetimes ago, fair Chavaleh, our actress. After a painful birth you gave me that name and promptly died. You were thirteen.

   *(***RANDI** *recoils with a sudden shiver.)*

PHIL. Now, hold it right there. What are you saying, that she–she was your mother?!

LUCIUS. Five times.

PHIL. This is crazy!

LUCIUS. *(To* **PHIL.***)* You were my wife eleven times.

PHIL. Mickey, cut this out, willya!?

LUCIUS. We will make far better progress if you will accept the fact that Michael, in your terms, is not here. As I said, he is resting comfortably.

PHIL. I gotta be losing my mind.

LUCIUS. *(Holds up his hand.)* A moment. *(He cocks his head as if listening to something.)* Yes... Michael wisely suggests that he make a brief appearance to assure you of his well being.

   *(***LUCIUS** *lowers himself onto the floor in lotus position, closes his eyes, takes a couple of deep breaths and lets his chin slowly drop to his chest. His breathing continues deep and evenly.)*

(After a few moments, he starts to gently flex his shoulders and neck as if coming out of slumber.)

(Now he opens his eyes and it's no longer **LUCIUS**-*it's* **MICKEY**.*)*

MICKEY. *(Blinks a few times.)* Wow... !

EVERYONE. Mickey...!

ANDY. Now *this* is Mickey!

*(***EVERYONE*** moves to* **MICKEY**, *except* **RANDI**.*)*

EMILY. Mickey, honey!

PHIL. Mick!

MICKEY. *(With a laugh.)* Hey...!

PHIL. Where were you, Mick?

*(***MICKEY*** lays his head on his hands and makes a "snoring" noise.)*

PHIL. Asleep.

MICKEY. Yeah.

ANDY. *(Looking at him closely.)* How do you feel, Mick?

MICKEY. *(Gives the claw to* **ANDY**'*s ribs.)* Rrrr!

ANDY. Yeah, yeah ...

EMILY. Are you all right, sweetie?

MICKEY. Oh, oh, oh...! *(Holds up the news ad and points to it.)*

ALL BUT RANDI. Next week, Mick.

ANDY. Does anyone remember normal breathing?

EMILY. I'm sure my hair is snow white by now.

RANDI. Andy, if this is a joke—

ANDY. A joke!

PHIL. If it's a joke, it's a mighty sick one.

ANDY. You guys, come on! We have to accept what's happening. It's unusual as hell, but it's happening. And I think it's okay, I really do. From the way this "person" talks, and what he tells us about the–the physical and psychological aspects, I really don't think we've got anything to be afraid of.

LUCIUS. Well said.

(*He's back! And* ANDY *springs to the other side of the room as if shot from a pistol. Everyone else jumps back as well.*)

ANDY. If he does that one more time...!

(PHIL *and* LUCIUS *rise together.* PHIL *staring at* LUCIUS *hard.*)

PHIL. You're not my son! Who are you? What have you done to my boy?

LUCIUS. I thought it would be obvious by now that I have done nothing to him.

PHIL. Nothing? Taking over his body; you call that nothing?

LUCIUS. If it will ease your mind, this interchange is being done with Michael's full blessing.

PHIL. His blessing. And just how did he manage to give that?

LUCIUS. Naturally it was given on a subconscious level.

PHIL. Oh, naturally. Now cut this out and answer my question. Who the hell are you?!

LUCIUS. In your terms, an old friend. (*Sits on couch in lotus position.*)

PHIL. You're no friend of mine. I never met you or anyone like you.

EMILY. We were friends?

PHIL. Don't you encourage him!

EMILY. Hush!

LUCIUS. Friends and enemies. Mothers and daughters. Fathers, brothers, master and slave, embezzlers, murderers, senators, holy men, paupers, prostitutes... the names and dates fade from importance; it is only the growth that matters.

PHIL. That's all... (*Heads for the closet; through this next he bundles up.*)

RANDI. (*Sarcastically.*) What kind of prostitute was I?

LUCIUS. Enthusiastic.

EMILY. You said you came to settle a debt.

PHIL. Quit talking to him!

EMILY. You mind your own business!

LUCIUS. A debt of gratitude. Gratitude for helping me to graduate from Classroom Earth. For you see, through centuries of our close interaction, I finally came to know myself. So now I would like to help you—*(Taking them all in.)*—who have chosen to sign on for a few more semesters, to see your lives with a fresh pair of eyes.

PHIL. Fresh eyes... terrific.

LUCIUS. I wish to spread some light.

PHIL. Now lights we could use.

EMILY. *(Finally notices* **PHIL.***)* Where are you going?

PHIL. Just keep your eye on Mickey 'til I get back. Can you do that one thing?

EMILY. *(Insistent.)* Where are you going?

PHIL. For some answers.

LUCIUS. Fetch a priest if you must, Philip. But my time grows short.

EMILY. A priest?!

ANDY. You're not getting a priest?!

PHIL. *(To* **LUCIUS.***)* What's your next trick, turning water into egg nog? Why don't you really impress me? Why don't you fix the electricity in this lousy house?

LUCIUS. Because I do not wish to deprive you of a valuable growth experience; that of learning to hire the appropriate craftsmen.

EMILY. You can't go bothering Father Corman; he's getting ready for midnight mass!

PHIL. I'd like to see somebody stop me.

EMILY. I'd like to see you get past Sister Cuthbert.

PHIL. What's she going to do, slap my hand with a ruler? My son is in trouble. I am going to get a priest here tonight if I have to hogtie him with his own rosary beads!

(Exits, slamming door.)

EMILY. *(After the dust settles.)* Well, maybe it's a good idea. Maybe we're not equipped to deal with this.

ANDY. Maybe. But I'm equipped to ask a few questions while Hurricane Phil is away. *(Sits on sofa arm.)* Lucius. Um... You're still Lucius, aren't you?

LUCIUS. Indeed.

EMILY. *(Suddenly; gasp!)* I never got you that coffee.

(Starts to move.)

ANDY. Mom–Mom. We'll do coffee later. *(she stays.)* Now, Lucius ...

RANDI. Andy–please.

ANDY. What?

RANDI. This is just a little too much right now.

ANDY. *(To* **LUCIUS.***)* She doesn't believe in you.

RANDI. No offense.

LUCIUS. None taken. As it is, your belief is not required.

RANDI. *(A beat.)* Required for what?

LUCIUS. My existence.

RANDI. ...How fortunate.

LUCIUS. But for what it is worth, I believe in you.

RANDI. *(Picks up newspaper.)* So, Andy, any good movies playing around here? *(The phone rings.)* "The Three Faces of Eve"? "Sybil"?

ANDY. *(Answers phone.)* Hello? ... Excuse me? ..."Shakey Joe's Bowl-a-Roma"?

RANDI. *(Suddenly.)* What?

ANDY. Uh... no, this isn't Shakey Joe's Bowl-a-Roma, you must have a wrong-

RANDI. Wait, wait! Shakey Joe's Bowl-a-Roma?!

ANDY. Yeah, why? *(Into phone.)* Hang on, maybe it is. *(To* **RANDI.***)* What?

RANDI. He's asking for Shakey Joe's Bowl-a-Roma?!

ANDY. Yes.

RANDI. *(Perplexed.)* Does Pittsburgh have one?

ANDY. I don't even know what it is!

RANDI. There couldn't be two! Ask him what he wants!

ANDY. What?

RANDI. Ask, ask!

ANDY. *(Sigh.)* Sir, what is it you want? *(To* **RANDI.***)* He wants to reserve a lane for New Year's Eve.

RANDI. *(Beside herself.)* He's got to be confused. Ask him where he's from!

ANDY. Whattaya mean where he's from?!

RANDI. Ask him where's he's calling from!

ANDY. You want to talk to him?

RANDI. Just ask, please?!

ANDY. Sir, may I ask where you're calling from? ...Rome? Rome, New York?

RANDI. *(Runs and grabs receiver from* **ANDY.***)* Excuse me, who is this? *(On hearing the answer she quickly hangs up, jumping away like the phone's haunted.)*

ANDY. What's the matter? Who was it?

RANDI. My father!

ANDY. What?!

RANDI. It was my father!

ANDY. Are you sure?

RANDI. It was my father!

ANDY. Well, why'd you hang up on him?

RANDI. Why? He wasn't calling me, he was calling Shakey Joe's. You heard him.

ANDY. Well, he got mixed up. Call him back.

RANDI. Mixed up?

ANDY. Yes.

RANDI. He dials Pittsburgh then asks for a bowling alley two blocks away from his house? He's crazy but he's not senile. Anyway, he doesn't have this number!

ANDY. You never gave it to him?

RANDI. I haven't spoken to the man in three years! ...Did you tell him?

ANDY. I haven't spoken to him in thirty-three years... You're dead certain that was your father?

RANDI. Yes! How did he sound to you? Nervous? Like he was up to something?

ANDY. No. Like he genuinely dialed a wrong number.

RANDI. Tell me how a man dials a one and an area code and seven specific numbers by pure chance!

LUCIUS. He doesn't.

(They stop and look at **LUCIUS.***)*

LUCIUS. Your father dialed his telephone correctly.

RANDI. Oh, is that so?

LUCIUS. The call was transferred here.

RANDI. How?

LUCIUS. *(Mock scary.) Boogie-boogie-boogie!*

RANDI. Give me a break!

ANDY. Perfect!

RANDI. Andy, stop. It's not even funny.... You believe him.

ANDY. So far it's the only thing that makes sense.

RANDI. Oh, bags of sense!

ANDY. Well, can you come up with an answer? I'd love to hear a more earthly explanation. Go ahead.

RANDI. He got your number somehow. Information.

EMILY. The operator won't give it out.

ANDY. How come?

EMILY. We're unlisted.

ANDY. See, we're– Why are we unlisted?

EMILY. Phil's good neighbor policy.

RANDI. *(To* **ANDY.***)* You gave him the number.

ANDY. Except that I didn't. How'd the phone call happen? *(No answer.)* Sunspots? A ventriloquist?

RANDI. What are you trying to get me to say, that I believe it was him?

ANDY. No, that you believe it was something. I'm not asking for the right answer. Just a theory.

RANDI. You're trying to deny me my right.

ANDY. What right?

RANDI. My right not to theorize.

ANDY. Randi, we're onto something new here! Everything that's happened here tonight. We're being let in on the ground floor. Can't you see it that way? Come on, this is a new world, explore it with me!

RANDI. Now we're Vikings.

ANDY. You don't feel the least bit of excitement? Like the tingle when you first discovered where babies come from?

RANDI. That was nausea.

ANDY. I'm not trying to get you to say something you don't believe. I just can't figure out what you believe.

RANDI. *(To* **EMILY.***)* When does he throw the baked apples?

ANDY. What does your gut tell you? How did that phone call happen?

RANDI. Drop it. Andy.

ANDY. I'm not asking how the universe happened, just the phone call.

RANDI. Leave me alone!

ANDY. I don't care what you believe, Randi, I'd just love to think that you believe something!

RANDI. Leave me alone! *(She exits quickly, running up the stairs.)*

ANDY. *(Moves to follow her up the stairs, but he stops and turns to* **EMILY.***)* I'm sorry...

EMILY. Go, go!

(ANDY exits. EMILY looks after them, concerned. But now She gets a gleam in her eye and looks at **LUCIUS.** *Almost giddy, she approaches him.)*

LUCIUS. *(Without looking up.)* You are bursting with questions.

EMILY. *(Eagerly.)* Do you have magical powers?

LUCIUS. True magic is merely the understanding of how nature operates, with a practical application of the rules.

EMILY. Was that a yes or a no?

LUCIUS. In your terms, yes, I have magical powers.

EMILY. *(Sits.)* Could you really straighten out the electricity in this house? I'm not asking you to do it. I just want to know if it's possible.

LUCIUS. It would be a simple matter of rearranging atoms.

EMILY. Rearranging.

LUCIUS. Rearranging.

EMILY. Amazing.

LUCIUS. What amazes is that the transfiguration of atoms for this and other purposes, such as the instantaneous transportation of matter, was at one time considered commonplace. It is how your earliest pyramids were erected. Now it is the stuff of fairy tales.

EMILY. You're joking with me.

LUCIUS. To do so would be fruitless and cruel.

EMILY. Man had such power?

LUCIUS. Man had such power.

EMILY. What stopped it?

LUCIUS. Man's love affair with fear. *(A moment.)* Question.

EMILY. *(Hesitantly.)* Do you think you could do something with Phil?

LUCIUS. You would like me to rearrange his atoms?

EMILY. *(Chuckles.)* No, no… But just a little something to get him to, well, to stop being grouchy, and stop griping about the neighbors and how the world's going to hell in a handbasket. Sometimes I think I'm going to lose my mind. I want… I want my fella back.

LUCIUS. *(After a pause.)* Grip your chair tightly, dear lady, for I am about to bowl you over with an obscure yet powerful cosmic truth.

(Nervously, **EMILY** *grips the chair.)*

LUCIUS. Ready? *(She nods. He takes a dramatic pause.)* That's life.

EMILY. What?

LUCIUS. Your husband has a perfect right to be grouchy and a perfect right to complain. But do you not realize that you have the right not to be subjected to his negativity? Where is it written that you must become involved in your husband's little dramas? To do so will not change him. If you are to change your husband then you need training.

EMILY. Anything. How do I train?

LUCIUS. Start small. Begin with something comparatively easy. Such as altering the course of your Mississippi River... Dear friend, people do not change until they are ready to change. Some never do.

EMILY. Then there's nothing I can do to help him?

LUCIUS. But, indeed. Let him know, often, that he is loved. *(A moment.)* Some advice: do not take things so seriously. It begins with a way of thinking. I presume to suggest that you simply think a little bit differently every day. And act a little differently. A little, mind you. Not this much a day–*(Spreading his arms wide.)*–but this much a day. *(Measuring an inch.)* And before even realizing it, you will have attained that highly prized yet elusive state of mind called "peace." *(A moment.)* The mechanism is tired. I will rest now.

EMILY. May I stay? I've never had a conversation with my son before. I think this is the closest I'm ever going to get.

LUCIUS. Perhaps you will consider having a conversation with your other son.

EMILY. Andy?

LUCIUS. Perhaps it is time he knew the truth about your Pirates of Pittsburgh. *(He closes his eyes and lowers his head.)*

(A pause.)

EMILY. *(Puzzled.)* My Pirates of... Pittsburgh.

(Suddenly she gasps, remembering a dark secret.)

Uh-oh... !

(The lights fade to black.)

Scene 4

(A short while later.)

*(****MICKEY*** *is sitting at the dining room table eating a piece of cake.)*

*(****EMILY*** *enters from the kitchen with a cup of steaming coffee.)*

EMILY. *(Re: the coffee.)* Finally!

*(Takes it to ****MICKEY*** *and sets it down before him.* ***MICKEY*** *looks at it indifferently.)*

EMILY. Now I suppose you don't want it.

MICKEY. Yechh!

EMILY. *(Taking it back to the kitchen.)* I wish you two would make up your minds. *(Exits.)*

*(Now ****ANDY*** *wearily descends the staircase. In the living room he stops and lets out a heavy, private sigh. Now he looks around the empty room and checks his watch.)*

ANDY. *(Calls out.)* How long can it take to kidnap a priest? *(He proceeds to the dining room, stopping at ****MICKEY****'s chair.)* Who's home?

MICKEY. *(Eating.)* Nnn.

ANDY. Mickey's home.... You're the star of the show, bro', how's it feel?

MICKEY. Nnn.

*(****ANDY*** *sits at the table.* ***EMILY*** *enters with a glass of milk.)*

EMILY. How's Randi?

*(****ANDY*** *makes a "so-so" gesture.* ***MICKEY*** *is reaching for his milk before ****EMILY*** *even gets near the table.)*

EMILY. All right, all right! *(To ****ANDY****.)* She lying down?

ANDY. Washing her face.

EMILY. Crying?

ANDY. Yeah. *(Reaches over and picks a bit of cake off of ****MICKEY****'s plate.)*

MICKEY. *(Not pleased.)* Nnn!

ANDY. Sorry. *(Puts it back.)* I forgot, you're eating for two now.

EMILY. Crying about what?

ANDY. Oh... her father, her sister... it's complicated.

EMILY. None of my business anyway.

(RANDI enters from upstairs.)

ANDY. Hi.

EMILY. Sit down, dear, I made you some tea.

RANDI. Thank you.... Mrs. Gorski, could I use your phone?

EMILY. Of course.

RANDI. *(Going to phone in living room.)* Thanks. It's long distance, but I'll pay you for it.

EMILY. Oh, don't be silly. *(EMILY exits into kitchen.)*

RANDI. *(Dials phone and waits.)* Daddy? Hi, it's Chava. Fine, thanks, how are you? Pittsburgh. Visiting. Oh? No kidding. No, couldn't have been me, I'm in Pittsburgh. Um... I just wanted to wish you and Mom a happy Chanukah. You're welcome.

(EMILY enters with tea things and goes to table.)

RANDI. Oh, everything's fine, how about you? Good. No, really, everything's fine. It's just been a long time.... I know.... Yeah.... Yeah, me too. Listen, I have to go but I'll write you a long letter real soon. Yeah, I promise. 'Kay, you too. 'Bye.

(Hangs up, walks to couch and sits. ANDY brings her teacup and kneels at her side.)

RANDI. Thanks. *(Takes a sip and sets cup down.)* He called Shakey Joe's and instead got a girl who sounded exactly like me. *(Fighting tears.)* Andy... if what's happening here tonight is really happening, then what makes sense anymore? What is logic? What's left to hold on to?

ANDY. *(Rubs her shoulder.)* I know... I know... What we've seen here isn't covered by yesterday's version of reality. So, I think we're going to have to do what they did in 1492.

RANDI. Please, Andy, I need for you to make sense right now.

ANDY. I am making sense.

RANDI. Yesterday's version of reality? Andy, reality is reality.

ANDY. Except look what happened in 1492. Reality was that the world was flat. It didn't matter that it was really round. Everyone believed it was flat so that was reality. Then along came Columbus and suddenly everyone had to—expand their version of reality to fit the new development. Well, we can do that, too. *(Re:* **MICKEY.***)* Honey, this feels so right to me. I can't toss it off just because I can't explain it.

RANDI. Well, I think it's beautiful that you can do that. But I can't. I'm scared. I want children.

ANDY. So do I.

RANDI. Great. But they're going to come to us one day, as all kids do, and they're going to say, "Mommy, what does God look like? Daddy, what happens when you die?" If we can't agree on one version of reality, Andy, what on earth do we tell them? What do we say?

ANDY. *(A pause.)* ...I don't know.

RANDI. I don't either.

ANDY. Guess we're... kinda lookin' at a whole new ball game, aren't we?

EMILY. *(Suddenly.)* Why'd you say that?

ANDY. Excuse me?

EMILY. Why'd you say ball game; why'd you say that?

ANDY. What do you mean, why'd I say that?

EMILY. It wasn't my idea, y'know. Phil was the one.

ANDY. The one what? What are you talking about?

EMILY. *(A pause.)* ...Nothing.

ANDY. Nothing? Are you alright?

EMILY. Nothing, I'm alright.

ANDY. 'Kay. *(Turns back to* **RANDI.***)*

EMILY. *(Suddenly.)* Did I know Georgie Thurman was going to become Georgie Thurman?

ANDY. Mom, what are you talking about?

EMILY. I swear to God, Andy, if I knew it meant he'd end up wearing an apron, babysitting cans of tuna fish, I would have made him take the Pirate's offer.

ANDY. *(Gently touches her hand.)* Who are you and what have you done with my mother?

EMILY. *(Slaps his hand.)* Stop that.

ANDY. Well, you're talking crazy! The Pirates' offer...

EMILY. Andy, how I wish you could have seen your father on that pitcher's mound! Strike one, strike two, strike three! And did that crowd go crazy! And me-well! I was a goner from the start.

ANDY. But what did you mean the Pirates?

EMILY. The Pittsburgh Pirates.

ANDY. I know what city! What offer?

EMILY. See, I knew I should have told you this before.

ANDY. Do you want me to burst a blood vessel? Tell me!

EMILY. It was a contract.

ANDY. A contract?

EMILY. For him and Georgie. Together. The owner called them up. He asked them to come in.

ANDY. You're standing there and telling me that the Pittsburgh Pirates wanted my father?

EMILY. I couldn't believe it, either. Imagine, he rushes home with all this wonderful news. But that was the thing, see. He rushed home and found me sitting on the front stoop.

ANDY. Wait, before the stoop! Give me a time frame. When are we talking?

EMILY. I'd just had Mickey.

ANDY. And I'm a baby, okay, go.

EMILY. And I was sitting on the stoop, see, 'cause I'd just come from the doctor and I forgot my key. So Phil sat down on the steps and told me all his wonderful news. Then I had to tell him my news–that Mickey wasn't a normal baby. Phil said galivanting all over the country wasn't any way to take care of a family. Not a special one like ours. That's when he went to see my brother, Harold. And Harold practically gave him that little grocery store, bless his soul. Saved our lives. But, then, Harold liked Phil. Everyone liked Phil.

(A moment.)

ANDY. You're not making this up. *(***EMILY*** gestures "no.")* Why was I never told this?

EMILY. Oh, Andy ...

ANDY. Daddy left baseball because he got hit by a car–that's the story I grew up with.

EMILY. Do you think your father could stand anyone feeling sorry for him? Because he did something nice? This way was easier, he could just blame some drunk driver from out of nowhere. Nobody needed to know. But now, well... a little bird told me that you needed to know.

ANDY. Y'know, I grow up with this man who's mad all the time... so I just figure he's mad at me.

EMILY. Now I wish I had told you. I'm so sorry.

ANDY. No, no, Mama, you did what you had to do. It's just... all these years I think I know this guy. The old crank in the basement who defies death every year, putting up Christmas lights. *(To himself.)* The Pittsburgh freaking Pirates... *(To* **EMILY.***)* Okay, now, would you finish the story? When did Dad actually get hit by the car?

EMILY. ....He never got hit by a car.

ANDY. *(Stunned for a moment.) Then how did he break his hip?!*

EMILY. Putting up the Christmas lights.

*(***ANDY*** falls back into this chair. This is too much! Now there is a commotion at the front door. Everyone turns to see a wet, frustrated and angry* **PHIL GORSKI** *enter, slamming the door behind him.)*

PHIL. *(Glowers at everyone.)* Electricians, plumbers, priests! The unions are killing this country!

(EMILY and MICKEY go to him as he hangs up his things. Through this next, PHIL will rummage through drawers and shelves, trying to find something.)

EMIL Y. What happened? Did you bring Father Corman?

PHIL. Yeah, Emily, I shrunk him and he's in my coat!

EMILY. Don't get smart!

PHIL. How's Mickey?

EMILY. What took you so long?

PHIL. How's Mickey?

EMILY. He's delightful!

ANDY. What happened, Dad?

PHIL. Before or after my Die-Hard battery kicked the bucket?

EMILY. Oh, that car!

PHIL. Sister Cuthbert had to jump-start me.

ANDY. Sorry I missed that.

EMILY. So what did Father Corman say?

PHIL. Well, I'll tell you this about Father Corman—he's no Mother Theresa. *(Finds a rosary; discreetly pockets it.)*

EMILY. What did he say?

PHIL. I quote– "Mr. Gorski, why a priest? Why not call a doctor?"

EMIL Y. Didn't you tell him the kind of things Mickey's been saying?

PHIL. And have him think I lost my marbles? I just told him Mickey started talking, that's all. I thought that would be enough. *(Finds a ten-inch wooden crucifix; hides it in his sweater.)*

EMILY. Okay, why don't we call a doctor?

PHIL. 'Cause we got three of 'em right here! And I'll be frank, you all stink! Now, out. Everybody out. Pile into the kitchen or someplace. Come on, let's go.

EMILY. What?

PHIL. *(To MICKEY.)* Exceptin' you.

MICKEY. Nnn.

PHIL. Out, now. All the doctors off the field. Hit the show-
ers. Let's move.

EMILY. What are you up to?

PHIL. My ears–in experts. Now it's my turn. Come on, up.

(EMILY, ANDY *and* RANDI *start to move.*)

ANDY. Dad, what are you going to do?

EMILY. What are you going to do to him?

PHIL. I'll let you know when I've done it. *(Herding them to
the kitchen.)* Now, come on. You might as well be where
there's food, 'cause this may take a long time.

EMILY. Will you answer me?

PHIL. Out!

EMILY. *(Tsk.)* Honest to God... *(Exits with* RANDI *into kitchen.)*

ANDY. Mickey, if things get rough... *(Makes the "claw.")* Rrr!

PHIL. Hey! Hey! Out!

(ANDY *exits into the kitchen. Now* EMILY *comes back out
and heads for the table.*)

PHIL. *(Snaps.)* Emily!

EMILY. *(Snaps back.)* I want my tea!

PHIL. Now, no matter what you hear, stay in there. I don't
care if it sounds like a bullfight out here. Just leave us
alone. Y'hear me?

EMILY. *(Deadpan.)* Ole'. *(She exits.)*

PHIL. *(Finally alone,* PHIL *turns and faces* MICKEY.*)* Now... !

MICKEY. Hey!

(PHIL *moves to the little table next to his chair and sets
the crucifix down.*)

MICKEY. *(Unimpressed.)* Nnn.

(PHIL *proceeds to a hanging portrait of the Blessed
Mother and plucks it from its spot on the wall.*)

MICKEY. *(Picks up crucifix like a toy airplane.)* Vvvvvvvv...

PHIL. *(Horrified.)* Mickey, no, no!

(MICKEY *giggles and sets it down.* PHIL *places the portrait next to it.*)

PHIL. *(PHIL goes hunting for something else. In the drawers, on the shelves–but he can't find it. Calls out.)* Emily, where's the Bible? *(No answer. He goes for the kitchen door just as* EMILY *pushes it open, banging him in the knee.)* Emil-OW!

EMILY. Oh, I'm sorry.

PHIL. It's okay, I'll use two canes! ...Where's the Bible?

EMILY. *(Like it's the first time she's heard the word.)* The Bible? *(PHIL moans.)* ...Oh, wait a minute. *(She disappears into the kitchen.* PHIL *waits. She returns and hands him a Bible.)* Here.

PHIL. What's it doing in the kitchen?

EMILY. Holding up my cookbooks.

PHIL. What the-? Why the Bible, for Christ's sake, what's the matter with you? Why not the phone book?

EMILY. We use the phone book. *(She exits.)*

(Now PHIL *puts the Bible with the other items. He gently guides* MICKEY *to sit in his chair. Now he discreetly puts the rosary around his neck, picks up the crucifix and stands nonchalantly with his back to* MICKEY.)

PHIL. *(Suddenly turns to* MICKEY, *brandishing the crucifix.)* All right, come out of there!

*(*MICKEY *giggles.)*

PHIL. Shh. Quiet, Mick.... Come on, I know you're in there.

(He giggles some more.)

PHIL. Mickey, go to sleep.

*(*MICKEY *makes a funny snoring noise, then laughs at his own joke.)*

PHIL. Mick, no, no, shh.

*(*MICKEY *gets quiet.)*

PHIL. Come on out... Come on. Before you do any more harm to my son you gotta deal with me, so let's go... Come on, you think I raised this kid up just so you could get your claws into him? Ha!

MICKEY. Ha!

PHIL. Mick, sit still, willya? He comes out when you're sitting still.

MICKEY. Nnn.

PHIL. *(Sets crucifix down and begins pacing.)* That's all right, I'll wait. I got all night. You come out, I'll be here. Oh, and don't think I don't know why you're here, pal. It hit me coming home in the car. Just another one of God's little punishments. "You messed up, Phil Gorski. You let son number one stray from the Church. You let him bring an atheist into your house." Okay, fine, yes, I did that. I did it all. *(To heaven.)* But that was me! Not him! *(He notices that the kitchen door is open a crack. He barks:)* Quit listenin'! *(The door slams shut! Back to* **LUCIUS**.*)* Now, come on out. Y'hear me? *(After more waiting, it begins to look like it's all for nothing.)* Y'hear me? Come on! *(But* **MICKEY** *remains* **MICKEY**.*)* *(Sigh.)* ...Mick, Mick.... I dunno. Maybe I should've put you in a home. Maybe they would've taken care of you better. Maybe none of this would've happened.

(Through this next, the kitchen door slowly opens. **RANDI** *quietly enters and stands unobtrusively against the wall. She is followed by* **ANDY**, *and eventually* **EMILY**. **PHIL** *sees none of this.)*

PHIL. Oh, God.... Please God, take this away from my son. Don't hurt him, he didn't do nothin'. Hurt me, wouldya? Take the other hip. Please, I can stand more pain. I'll take whatever you dish out.

LUCIUS. I spoke with God this morning.

*(***PHIL** *watches as* **LUCIUS** *moves to window and looks up at the stars.)*

LUCIUS. I warned Him of a crisis situation in the Pleiades star system. At the rate the planet Skartaris is deviating from its orbit, it is only a matter of days before it collides with the third moon of Maladeck, causing chaos and destruction to its cosmic neighbors. *(A pause.)* God said He was unable to deal with it as He was busy making sure that Phil Gorski was receiving the correct amount of pain today. *(Turns to* **PHIL**.*)* Dear troubled man, what kind of a Creator have you created, who would inflict his children with pain simply because they stumbled through life as best they knew how?

PHIL. Blasphemy just pours out of you like a tapped keg, don't it? God don't give me nothing I don't deserve. Says so right here, pal. *(Picks up Bible.)* But you probably never heard of this book.

LUCIUS. Indeed. I have read the original.

PHIL. The original? What do you call this, a K-Mart special?

LUCIUS. Your holy book still holds much truth.

PHIL. *Much* truth? The whole truth, buddy, and nothing but the truth!

LUCIUS. Diluted, edited, censored, distorted... mostly with good intentions, but sometimes by those who sought to rule a populace by striking fear into their hearts.

PHIL. You just get better and better. You actually want me to believe that?

LUCIUS. Certainly not. It would be better if you did your own research. You have resources. But mostly you have a heart that will tell you what is right and what is not so right. Listen to it. *(Sits on floor.)*

RANDI. What if all I get is dead air?

PHIL. *(Startled.)* Hey! Excuse me, but this is private! Get back in there, all of you!

RANDI. *(Ignores* **PHIL**.*)* How many times do I have to ask why an innocent child was killed before I get an answer?

PHIL. Andy, would you please?

ANDY. He's here for her, too, Dad.

RANDI. *(To* **LUCIUS**.*)* And don't tell me God took her because He wanted her with Him in heaven. If I hear that one again I'll scream.

LUCIUS. No. Those answers will no longer satisfy in this new age.

PHIL. There it is! "New Age!" If I hear that one again *I'll* scream!

LUCIUS. When you are through screaming, open your eyes. And behold a world coming out of its adolescence. You are standing on the threshold of something quite exciting in the history of humankind. Now, you can complain and pine for the old days, or you can dig your feet in and enjoy it. It is up to you.

RANDI. *(To* **ANDY.***)* He's not going to answer my question.

LUCIUS. Not with an answer you'll like.

RANDI. Try me.

LUCIUS. I will suggest that there is no such thing as an innocent victim; that, as a soul, your sister had more to do with her own death, and her own birth, than you suspect.

RANDI. Look... I like you... you have lovely ideas. But right now I need a little less philosophy, and a lot more reality.

LUCIUS. Ah, reality. Come close.

(Reluctantly, she moves closer to **LUCIUS.** *He gestures for her to come down to his level. She kneels.)*

LUCIUS. Why do you suppose so many people in your world lead mixed up lives? I'll tell you. It is because they look at the mixed up mess that's all around them and they say, "There now. See? That's reality. That's what I'm about." *(A little smile.)* That's not what you're about. Reality is right in there. *(Points to her heart.)* That is where you'll find your answers. And if you can't hear them it is because you have allowed everyone else's clatter to drown them out.

PHIL. *(Rises.)* Alright, enough with your clatter and your New Age and your exciting thresholds-just leave my son alone! Get out!

EMILY. Phil!

PHIL. What's the matter, don't you want your son back? I want him back. *(To* **LUCIUS.***)* So what's it gonna take? You can't have a priest, we're all out of priests tonight But you got me! Now what else do we need here, some holy water? I can get you a barrelful. Prayers? I know 'em all.

ANDY. *(Moves to* **PHIL.***)* Dad ...

PHIL. Incense? Name your flavor.

ANDY. *(Touches* **PHIL.***)* Dad... *(***PHIL** *is taken off guard by* **ANDY***'s touch.)* ...Have a little faith. It's going to be alright.

RANDI. *(Rises.)* Mr. Gorski?

PHIL. No, please, miss, just stay out of this!

RANDI. Why don't you just try asking him?

PHIL. Asking him what?

RANDI. To leave.

> *(***PHIL** *stares at* **RANDI.** *then turns to* **LUCIUS** *and contemplates the idea.)*

RANDI. ...Nicely.

PHIL. *(He takes his time about it. It's a radical concept.)* ... *(Ahem.)* Will you leave? ...Nicely?

LUCIUS. Goodbye. *(He lowers his head.)*

> *(They stare at the silent, still* **LUCIUS.***)*

PHIL. *(Takes a careful step closer.)* Whattaya think?

ANDY. I think it's goodbye.

EMILY. *(Sadly.)* For good?

PHIL. I'll get you a cat.

> *(Now they wait for* **MICKEY** *to wake up as his old self. But it's taking a long time.)*

PHIL. Alright, alright, come on.

ANDY. Dad, be patient.

EMILY. No, something's wrong.

ANDY. How can you tell?

LUCIUS. *(Suddenly jerks to life.)* Due to circumstances...

EMILY. I knew it!

LUCIUS ....beyond our control... there will be a delay in Michael's return.

ANDY. What's the matter?

LUCIUS. *(Now his words come with a noticeable effort.)* An energy depletion... plus the mechanism's inherent

limitations... are making... an already complex maneu-
ver... even more...

ANDY. Okay, take it easy. Relax.

LUCIUS. I had... questioned the wisdom of... using this
vehicle.... But Michael's... fervent request was... so irre-
sistible...

ANDY. Michael's–? Michael's request? What does that
mean? What did Mickey request?

LUCIUS. Me.

ANDY. You? You mean he asked you to come?

EMILY. *(To* LUCIUS.*)* This thing wasn't your idea?

(LUCIUS *gestures "no," then lowers his head and sits
silently.)*

ANDY. But *why* did he ask for you?

PHIL. Alright, enough, shh-shh! *(Gestures for* ANDY *to leave*
MICKEY *be.* ANDY *reluctantly moves away.)*

ANDY. *(To* EMILY.*)* Mickey asked him to come! Why?
(Perplexed, EMILY *shrugs.* ANDY *approaches* MICKEY *again.)*
...He can't leave now.

PHIL. *(Gestures* ANDY *away.)* No-no-no ... !

ANDY. But if there's more to this...

PHIL. Leave him be!

(ANDY *retreats back to* EMILY.*)*

ANDY. ...Mom, why would Mickey arrange this? Why would
he want to shake up his family like this? Why?

EMILY. I don't know.

ANDY. Especially on Christmas. *(Turns to her.)* Is that it?
'Cause it's Christmas?

EMILY. What?

ANDY. And we're all together? ...No, we were all together
last year. What's different now?

EMILY. You brought a girl home.

ANDY. I've brought girls home before. What's different?

EMILY. *(A pause.)* It's this girl.

(ANDY *grabs* EMILY'*s face and kisses it. He now goes to* RANDI, *who is seated, and kneels before her.*)

ANDY. *(Takes her hands.)* And with this girl comes the question–are the old ways worth holding onto just because they're old? Do some ideas deserve rethinking? *(A pause.)* Randi... when our kids come to us, and they start asking those big questions, about life and death and God... let's give them something we never had– the chance to make up their own minds.

PHIL. Whoa, whoa! That's rethinking?

ANDY. Because no matter what we tell them, in thirty years they'll be asking the same questions all over again.

RANDI. That's the best idea I've heard all day.

(Now MICKEY *captures everyone's attention, for he is shuddering severely.*)

PHIL. Mickey?

(*The shuddering quickly grows into violent and spasmodic shaking.* MICKEY *is clearly in the throes of a convulsion.*)

ANDY. *(Runs to* MICKEY.) Jesus! Mickey!

PHIL. What's going on?!

ANDY. Has this happened before?

EMILY. Never! Help him, Andy!

ANDY. *(Snatches Mickey's flailing arms.)* Mick!

(MICKEY'*s reflex action is a violent shove which sends* ANDY *sprawling onto the floor.* EMILY *screams.* ANDY *sits up and shakes his head clear.* MICKEY'*s convulsion worsens.* ANDY *makes another pass at him.*)

ANDY. Mick! Easy, Mick, shh-shh-shh, Mick-

(*He grabs* MICKEY'*s wrists, pulls him to his feet and wraps his arms around him. But* MICKEY *will not tolerate anyone's touch and with a mighty heave he throws* ANDY *clear of him.* MICKEY *falls to the floor and continues writhing.*)

EMILY. Andy... !

ANDY. Damnit, he's strong!

PHIL. *(Approaches* **MICKEY.***)* Mickey...!

ANDY. Don't Dad! Mom, call an ambulance!

EMILY. *(Running for phone.)* Oh my God!

PHIL. Nine-one-one, Emily! Hurry up!

ANDY. He can't make the transition!

MICKEY. *(With a Herculean effort he stops convulsing long enough to dig his nails into the carpet, lift his head and let out a low, guttural* **LUCIUS** *voice.)* He-e-elp hi-i-im!

EMILY. *(Screams.)* Mickey!

(Now **MICKEY** *is abruptly seized and hurled back into his convulsion.)*

(At this, **RANDI** *leaps into the fray, making a lunge for* **MICKEY***'s shirt pocket. She is instantly knocked aside by another of* **MICKEY***'s wild swings. But she is back in a flash and manages to pin his arm while wrestling the newspaper out of his pocket.)*

RANDI. *(Once she's got the paper she endeavors to hold it before his shaking, contorted face while pinning his quaking body to the floor.)* Wrestling, Mick! Wrestling! Wrestling! Wrestling! Mickey, wrestling, Mick! Next week, Mick! Next week! Next week! Wrestling! *(It's working.)* Wrestling, Mick, wrestling. Next week, Mickey. Huh, sweetie? Huh? Wrestling matches next week? Huh?

(The convulsions gradually fade. She gingerly touches his shoulder, then strokes his head while the family watches, spellbound.)

Okay, Mickey? Huh? Wrestling? You and Daddy? Huh? You and Daddy?

(Finally **MICKEY** *is still and breathing evenly. Soon he blinks his eyes open.)*

MICKEY. *(Softly.)* Wow...!

(The family breathes a sigh of relief.)

RANDI. *(Stroking* **MICKEY***'s head.)* How are ya, pal?

MICKEY. Hey!

RANDI. What is this, Mick? Wrestling?

MICKEY. Oh boy!

> *(The family gathers around.* **PHIL** *takes* **MICKEY** *by the hand.)*

PHIL. Up, Mick, come on. Here we go. That's it.

> *(***MICKEY** *stands up.* **ANDY** *lifts* **RANDI** *to her feet and hugs her ferociously.)*

PHIL. *(To* **MICKEY**.*)* How are ya? Y'alright?

> *(***MICKEY** *giggles.* **PHIL** *hugs him.)*

PHIL. Mick, listen to me. Don't go away anymore, huh? Please? Will you do that for me? Just stay put, huh? 'Cause we all miss you when you go. Okay?

MICKEY. Nnn.

EMILY. Let me kiss this girl's wonderful face.

ANDY. *(Still hugging* **RANDI**.*)* The line forms on the right.

> *(***EMILY** *gets her head between them and kisses* **RANDI**. *Now* **MICKEY** *leaves* **PHIL**'s *embrace and walks over to* **RANDI**.*)*

MICKEY. Hey.

RANDI. Hey, yourself.

> *(***MICKEY** *puts out his hand. She goes to shake it but* **MICKEY** *pulls a switch, giving her the claw in the side.)*

MICKEY. Rrr!

> *(***RANDI** *yelps and leaps into* **ANDY**'s *arms.* **ANDY** *laughs.)*

EMILY. There's gratitude.

MICKEY. *(To* **EMILY**.*)* Rrr!

EMILY. *(Hugs* **MICKEY**.*)* Andy, I still think we should have a doctor look at him.

ANDY. Me too, Mom.

EMILY. What do you think, Phil?

PHIL. *(Has been standing off by himself.)* Oh... yeah, sure.

(Holds out his arm.) Jesus, lookit... my hair's still standing up. I thought he was a goner. Honest to God.

EMILY. *(Goes to* **PHIL.** *)* Are you alright?

PHIL. Yeah, yeah.... Mickey's life flashed before my eyes.

EMILY. Mickey's life? It's supposed to be your own life.

PHIL. Never mind, I know what I saw. *(A moment.)* Hey, whattaya say, folks? Let's get the hell outa this nutty house. *(Checks watch.)* If we move our tails we can just make midnight mass.

EMILY. Midnight mass, holy mackerel! *(Runs for stairs.)* All this talk about God, how am I supposed to remember church? *(She exits up the stairs.)*

*(***ANDY*** takes* **MICKEY** *to closet and through this next helps him into his coat.)*

PHIL. Hey, Randi with an i, ever been to a midnight mass?

RANDI. No.

PHIL. Well, you might like it. There'll be parts you won't get, but... But I don't get why your men wear beanies, so it all evens out. You'll like the singing, anyway. Andy used to sing in the choir, he can tell you. Andy had a beautiful voice.

ANDY. You never told me that.

PHIL. *(Gruffly.)* Well, I'm telling you now. *(To* **RANDI.** *)* So, what the hell? Wanna join us?

(There is a moment between them.)

RANDI. What the hell? *(Now she gives him a quick kiss on the cheek. She joins* **ANDY** *at the closet.)*

PHIL. *(Smiles to himself; shouts.)* Two minutes to twelve, Emily! Coats, coats!

EMILY. *(From upstairs.)* I am not deaf!

PHIL. Midnight mass, Mick. How 'bout that?

MICKEY. How are ya?

(At this, **PHIL** *and* **ANDY** *look at* **MICKEY** *in astonishment,)*

PHIL. What?!

MICKEY. How are ya?

PHIL. How are ya?

ANDY. *(In disbelief)* How are ya?

MICKEY. How are ya?

PHIL. *(Excited.)* Emily!

EMILY. *(Coming down stairs with her hat and coat.)* What?

PHIL. C'mere!

EMILY. What's the matter?

PHIL. Listen to this! ... Mick, *how are ya?*

MICKEY. How are ya?

EMILY. *(Gasp!)* Mickey!

MICKEY. How are ya?

EMILY. *(Overjoyed.)* How are ya? Well! *(Hugs* **MICKEY.***)*

PHIL. I been trying to get him to say that for years! Mick, how are ya?

MICKEY. How are ya?

(They all laugh with delight.)

PHIL. Good for you, fella. Now, you say that to Father Corman, Mick. I told him you've been talking!

*(***EMILY*** *hands* **PHIL** *his coat and then gives him a good, solid no nonsense kiss on the lips.)*

PHIL. *(He's thrown. Then confidentially.)* What the hell's that?!

EMILY. It's acting a little bit differently every day.

PHIL. *(Gives her a look like she's half crazy-but he likes it.)* Yeah, well... Come on, everybody.

EMILY. I just want to leave a light on.

PHIL. *(Opening door.)* We haven't missed a midnight mass in thirty-five years and I'm not about to—

EMILY. *(Whoops!* **EMILY** *has flipped a light switch and plunged the entire house into darkness, window decorations and all.)* Oops!

PHIL. Jesus, Mary and Joseph!

ANDY. Dad has a curse for every major holiday.

EMILY. Mama did it again, huh Mickey?

ANDY. I'll go down to the basement. Where's the flashlight?

PHIL. No, no, we'll be late for mass. Let's go.

EMILY. My turkey will spoil!

PHIL. Not in one hour. Come on.

EMILY. Wait, I can't find my sleeve.

PHIL. Here, gimme the coat... Ow! ...You're battin' a thousand tonight, Emily.

(Now, little by little, slowly, slowly, the bulbs on the Christmas tree start to light up.)

EMILY. I'm sorry. Where did I hit you?

PHIL. You have to know now? ...Hey, I hear kissing!

ANDY. You do not.

PHIL. It's kissing or you're cleaning a drain over there.

(Now everyone notices the tree as the lights continue to glow brighter and brighter.)

PHIL. What the hell–?!

(The growing light now reveals our friends huddled at the doorway, coats half-on, half-off, all watching the tree, frozen in a stunned tableau.)

MICKEY. Wow...!

RANDI. H–how's it doing that?!

PHIL. Who plugged it in? Somebody plugged it in.

ANDY. No they didn't Anyway, the electricity's off.

PHIL. Not over there it's not. Check the plug.

*(**ANDY** approaches the tree.)*

PHIL. Be careful

ANDY. Don't worry. *(Keeping his distance from the tree, he feels around on the floor for the plug.)*

PHIL. I shoulda had my head examined buying this house.

*(Now, in amazement, **ANDY** slowly lifts the end of the cord. It is clearly not plugged into anything.)*

(The lights are now up to their peak of brightness, bathing the room in a warm glow.)

PHIL. It's not possible.

RANDI. Except there it is.

EMILY. *(Sing-songy.)* I know who's doing it...

PHIL. No! Geddada here...

RANDI. Do you think it's dangerous?

ANDY. No.

> *(Whenever anyone moves now it's with eyes glued to the wondrous tree.* ANDY *and* RANDI *sit together on the floor.)*

EMILY. He wanted to spread some light

PHIL. Huh?

EMILY. *(Sits on sofa.)* Do you think we could miss midnight mass this year?

PHIL. I guess we could go in the morning.... Mick, gimme your hand.

MICKEY. How are ya?

> *(PHIL takes MICKEY's hand and starts for the tree. PHIL sits on arm of sofa next to EMILY. MICKEY sits on the floor in the midst of them all.)*

PHIL. Got anything like this in New York?

> *(ANDY smiles at PHIL.)*

RANDI. Mr. and Mrs. Gorski, it's the most beautiful tree I've ever seen.

PHIL. Thanks.

EMILY. A simple matter of rearranging atoms.

> *(The curtain falls)*

THE END

COSTUME PLOT

Phil Gorski

Shirt: ivory
Sweater: burgundy cardigan
Trousers: brown
Suspenders: brown
Belt: brown
Shoes: brown loafers
Socks: brown
T-shirt
Reading glasses
Christmas bow tie
Parka: navy blue
Hat: grey fedora

Mickey/Lucius

Shirt: blue-grey plaid
Jeans
Suspenders: red
High-top Converse sneakers
Socks: sport
Jacket navy blue
Scarf: brown striped

Andy Gorski

Shirt: blue chambray
Sweater vest: Blue & olive "Fair Isle"
Tie: blue silk
Sports jacket: green glen-plaid
Trousers: olive corduroy
Belt: brown
Socks: olive
Shoes: brown suede
Scarf: camel
Trench coat: tan

Emily Gorski

Dress: green & red

Slip

Hose

Shoes: Navy

Necklace

Corsage

Chrisbnas apron

Half-glasses

Coat: red quilted

Hat and scarf: red

Randi Stein

Jacket: velvet print

Knit top: coral

Skirt: black wool

Tights: black

Shoes: black

Hat: black

Coat: black & white check

Handbag: black

PROPERTIES PLOT

Furniture

    Dining room table and six chairs
    Sideboard
    Two arm chairs
    Sofa
    Ottoman
    End table
    Small table for creche
    Encyclopedia bookcase
    Hall table
    Coat rack

Preset onstage

  On dining room table:
    Runner
    Poinsettia plant

  In sideboard:
    Christmas tablecloth
    Napkins
    Napkin rings
    Crucifix
    Portrait of "Blessed Virgin Mary"

  On sideboard:
    Two candlesticks

  Hall table:
    Table lamp

  Creche table:
    Partial set-up of creche
    Bag on floor with remaining pieces

  On encyclopedia bookcase:
    Telephone
    Pittsburgh phone book
    Clock

Preset Offstage

In kitchen:

    4 wine glasses

    4 water glasses

    Cup for Mickey

    4 knives

    9 spoons

    5 forks

    5 salad bowls

    5 dinner plates

    Salt & pepper

    Sugar bowl & creamer

    Casserole (baked apples)

    Serving spoon

    Glass of milk

    2 coffee cups

    Cookie plate

    Water pitcher

    Teapot

    Bible

    Meatloaf*

    Mashed potatoes*

    Peas*

    Lettuce*

    Baked apples*

     *(Served in blackout)

In basement:

    2 boxes of Lionel trains

    Shopping bag with Christmas tree decor including a loose bulb, loose piece of garland and a box of ornaments with one broken

Upstage prop table:

   2 pieces of luggage
   Bag of airline peanuts and make-up in Randi's handbag
   Wrestling ad for Mickey

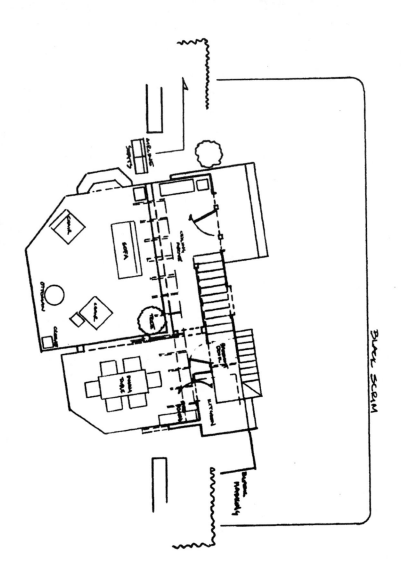

OTHER TITLES AVAILABLE FROM SAMUEL FRENCH

BEASLEY'S CHRISTMAS PARTY

C. W. Munger

Holiday Comedy / 2m, 1f (w/doubling) or 10m, 2f (w/o doubling)

Based on a story by Booth Tarkington. A journalist new to a Midwestern state capitol circa 1900 notices there is something funny going on at the charming house next door. Turns out gubernatorial candidate David Beasley lives there with his young ward, an orphan who has a menagerie of imaginary friends. Beasley's nemesis Simeon Peck plans to ruin Beasley's chances at the statehouse, but everyone learns something at *Beasley's Christmas Party* – including the pretty Miss Applethwaite, who Mr. Beasley spurned years before. Conceived for three actors to play multiple roles (but playable in many configurations), this 75-minute holiday play is a heartwarming fable of imagination and celebration.

"There's a goodhearted intelligence [to these characters]…with utter devotion to craftsmanship, they're distracting us from the play's age until we, without realizing, have been enchanted by it… Impressive as any number of rabbit-filled top hats…Enchanting."
– *Variety*

"In the holiday chests of many households, nestled in jumbles of ornaments and lights, there is one special heirloom, to be given pride of place on the Christmas tree: an old painted angel, perhaps, with history in its chipped wooden wings, or a faded star that outshines any flashy electric bulb. *Beasley's Christmas Party* is a bit like such small treasures." – *Time Out New York*

"A tiny seasonal treat (that) builds to an irresistibly charming climax…that good and bad always stay true, with good usually coming out ahead."– Michael Feingold, *Village Voice*

"A heartwarming tribute to the holiday season that adds a new touch of warmth and cheer to the Christmas season in these troubled times." – *Curtain Up*

OTHER TITLES AVAILABLE FROM SAMUEL FRENCH

A 1940'S RADIO CHRISTMAS CAROL

Walton Jones, David Wohl and Faye Greenberg

Musical Comedy / 6m, 3f, 2 optional characters for larger casts

The long-awaited sequel to the popular *The 1940's Radio Hour*. It's Christmas Eve, 1943, and the Feddington Players are now broadcasting from a hole-in-the-wall studio in Newark, NJ, and set to present their contemporary "take" on Dickens's *A Christmas Carol*. Whether it's the noisy plumbing, missed cues, electrical blackouts, or the over-the-top theatrics of veteran actor, but radio novice, William St. Claire, this radio show is an entertaining excursion into the mayhem and madness of a live radio show. St. Claire's escalating foibles and acting missteps propel the show to a simultaneously comedic and heart-wrenching dramatic climax: St. Claire has an on-air breakdown, and begins to connect his own life with that of the classic Dickens tale. In order to "save the show," the company improvises an ending to Charles Dickens' classic as a film noir mystery, featuring a hard-boiled detective, a femme fatale, and an absurd rescue of Tiny Tim (and the Lindbergh baby) from the clutches of a Hitler-esque villain named Rudolf! High School Musical lyricist Faye Greenberg and composer David Wohl have written four delightful period songs for the Feddington Players, and swing arrangements of many Christmas standards. Seamlessly combining drama and comedy, heartbreak and hope, The 1940's Radio Christmas Carol will sing its way into your heart. If you enjoyed 1940's Radio Hour, step back in time once again with the Feddington Players, and get into the holiday spirit with *The 1940's Radio Christmas Carol*.

"A reading that transforms Charles Dickens's classic into a gumshoe mystery...far above the usual holiday offerings."
–Stacy Nick, *Coloradoan*

OTHER TITLES AVAILABLE FROM SAMUEL FRENCH

JUDY'S SCARY LITTLE CHRISTMAS

Book by David Church and Jim Webber
Music and Lyrics by Joe Patrick Ward

Holiday Musical Comedy / 7m, 6f / Simple Set

Judy Garland is primed for her biggest comeback ever - the dazzling star of her own TV special, broadcast live on Christmas Eve, 1959. Judy's guests include Bing Crosby (making some holiday "grog"), Ethel Merman (plugging her Hawaiian album), and Liberace (with a handsome sailor in tow). However, mysterious snafus behind the scenes and cameo appearances by commie-baiting Vice President Richard Nixon (who performs a magic act) and blacklisted writer, Lillian Hellman, (who's forced to read "Children's Letter to Santa" with a puppet) throw Judy's program off course. The surprises climax when the arrival of Joan Crawford is interrupted by the spectral figure of...Death. The evening takes a detour into the twilight zone as the celebrities are forced to confront the lies behind their legends. Devastated and alone, Judy meets a special fan who ultimately proves that, despite her flaws, her shining legacy still endures.

"Magical! A side-splitting musical parody...wickedly funny!"
– *Los Angeles Times*

"Fascinating, hilarious and wildly entertaining!"
– Gerard Alessandrini, Creator of *Forbidden Broadway*

"Wonderfully strange...a true holiday treat!"
– *Hollywood Reporter*

"A non-stop hoot!"
– *Back Stage West*

"Hilarious! A surreal snow globe highball; a Hollywood Christmas card from beyond the grave!"
– *Portland Mercury*

CPSIA information can be obtained at www.ICGtesting.com
Printed in the USA
BVOW03s1542100914

366296BV00009B/113/P